I can't lose her....

David gunned the engine, trailing Laurel's car.

When he drew up behind her, her brake lights winked at him in a pair of short bursts. A deliberate move. She wasn't trying to lose him. She needed help.

Redness edged David's vision. If he got to this guy before the cops— No, he couldn't let fury cloud his mind. He clamped down on his emotions.

Laurel turned into a mall entrance and he signaled to follow, but another vehicle surged in front of him. Just that fast, he lost her.

Eternal seconds later, as he drove around to the other side of the lot, his heart leaped. There was her car, the driver's door wide-open.

David slammed on the brakes and ran to her car. Empty!

He stared wildly around, but saw nothing. His shoulders slumped. When she needed him the most, he'd failed the woman who meant more to him than his next heartbeat.

Why did he realize how precious she was now—when he might never get the chance to tell her?

Books by Jill Elizabeth Nelson

Love Inspired Suspense

Evidence of Murder
Witness to Murder
Calculated Revenge
Legacy of Lies
Betrayal on the Border
Frame-Up

JILL ELIZABETH NELSON

writes what she likes to read—faith-based tales of adventure seasoned with romance. By day she operates as housing manager for a seniors' apartment complex. By night she turns into a wild and crazy writer who can hardly wait to jot down all the exciting things her characters are telling her, so she can share them with her readers. More about Jill and her books can be found at www.jillelizabethnelson.com. She and her husband live in rural Minnesota, surrounded by the woods and prairie and their four grown children, who have settled nearby.

FRAME-UP

JILL ELIZABETH NELSON

HARLEQUIN® LOVE INSPIRED® SUSPENSE

Recycling programs
for this product may
not exist in your area.

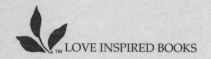

™ LOVE INSPIRED BOOKS

ISBN-13: 978-0-373-67590-6

FRAME-UP

www.Harlequin.com

Printed in U.S.A.

Charm is deceptive, and beauty is fleeting;
but a woman who fears the Lord is to be praised.
—*Proverbs* 31:30

To all who have passed through the fire of testing and chosen the high road with God, who makes them over in His image; to all the single parents committed to raising their children right in a "gone wrong" world.

ONE

"Mo-o-om! Look out for the ditch!"

Caroline's squeal rippled like a minor earthquake down Laurel Adams's spine. Her death grip on the steering wheel shot pain up her forearms as she hauled the car away from the telltale crunch of gravel beneath the tires.

She squinted into the smothering blanket of white. Faint streaks of yellow winked on her left-hand side. Yes, she was again in her driving lane.

A long breath eased from her throat as she let up another notch on the accelerator. They were crawling along at barely thirty-five miles per hour. She navigated more by feel than by sight. At least it was daytime—the middle of the afternoon, actually, though only her watch gave much assurance that the sun was overhead somewhere.

None of the news services had predicted this pre-Thanksgiving storm in the Rocky Mountains that had swooped out of nowhere and swallowed them in its howling maw. If she'd had any warning, she would have cancelled her speaking engagement at YMCA of the Rockies, stayed snug in Denver and dealt with her daughter's attitude in the comfort of their own home.

"Can't we turn around and go back?" Caroline's mocha-brown gaze pleaded with her mother.

"I'm sorry, sweetie." Laurel shook her head. "We must be getting close to Estes Park. It's safer to try to get that far and take shelter than to head home and hope we drive out of the storm."

Caroline scowled and let out a loud sniff. The girl had made no secret that she didn't want to come along on her mom's speaking engagement to the "praying and graying set." She'd begged to stay with their next door neighbor Janice, Laurel's best friend, like she often did when her mother traveled. Laurel hadn't consented this time, for her daughter's own good—or so she'd thought. In twenty-twenty hindsight, Caroline physically safe with Janice trumped Laurel's intention to use this trip as an opportunity for a heart-to-heart.

She spared a glance toward the teenager's sullen profile. Caroline was blooming into a pretty young woman, but at the moment she was more the pouty child. The girl's dark expression drew lines across her high forehead beneath a sleek cap of honey-blond hair and pinched a slender, straight nose into a sharp beak.

Laurel swallowed a sigh. The onset of hormonal ping-pong, normal for a girl newly thirteen years of age, couldn't be entirely to blame for the souring of her daughter's formerly sunny disposition. The downhill spiral had begun a few months ago, about the time Caroline's best friend moved away.

"I know you miss Emily," Laurel said, "but that doesn't mean you can let your schoolwork suffer. That D in biology has to improve after Thanksgiving vacation."

Caroline groaned.

"Oh, come on, sweetheart. Buck up! You're not alone in the world, you know. You have a solid support system. We can get you a tutor, if you need one, or a study group. In fact, something like that might be a chance for you to get out of your shell and make new friends."

"Is that what your psychologist mind is telling you? That I've suddenly developed abandonment issues?" Caroline's gaze narrowed. "If I didn't freak out when my dad left us when I was three and never looked back, why would I lose it because Emily moved to Tulsa? I talk to her on the phone and online nearly every day."

Laurel fixed her attention straight ahead, words churning for release behind her lips. What could she say that would pop the cork on whatever festered inside her daughter's heart? In her speaker persona, Laurel was touted as the voice of calm wisdom to beleaguered single parents everywhere, but right now she didn't have a clue how to deal with her own daughter.

Caroline threw her arms around herself. "Just for the record, Ms. Eldon is a head case. If you want to shrink someone, pick on her."

"Your biology teacher? Is she hard to talk to when you need help in class? I met her at parent-teacher conferences. She seemed cool and aloof, but very knowledgeable."

"Just your type, then." Caroline waved a dismissive hand. "I'm sure you two hit it off."

If her daughter had spewed curses at her, the pain would have been more bearable. Is that how Caroline saw her mother? Detached? Distant? Laurel worked hard at being reasonable…approachable, especially with her daughter.

Laurel swallowed and raised her chin. "Ms. Eldon's personality isn't the issue here. Your grades are important, young lady. You don't have to like your teacher in order to do your schoolwork. This getaway to the mountains—away from distractions—should provide time for you to buckle down and study."

"Only if we get there ali—" A scream rent Caroline's words.

Laurel echoed her daughter as something large and dark darted out of the ditch and paused in front of them. She hit the brakes and the shuddering car skidded into a doughnut on the snow-glazed roadway. Laurel's stomach leaped into her lungs, and her pulse jackhammered.

Help, God!

The car abruptly crunch-slid to a halt on the gravel verge facing the wrong way on the wrong side of the road. A few thuds from the trunk told of their luggage shifting. Laurel sat, staring straight ahead, arms rigid, fingers melded to the steering wheel. The creature that had been on the road in front of them was gone.

Caroline whimpered. "What was that thing?"

"Probably a deer." Laurel inhaled long and hard, sucking her stomach back into her abdomen. "We can thank God we're not stuck in the ditch."

"Or smashed at the bottom of a cliff."

"That, too."

"Or wrapped around a tree." The girl's tone edged toward hysteria. "I don't think we can make it to Estes Park."

"We're going to be fine, baby girl." Laurel made herself speak firmly, confidently, like she addressed the audiences for her speaking engagements. *God, help me keep that promise.*

Had Laurel dragged Caroline on this trip only to kill her—kill them both? The bass roar of the ceaseless wind taunted her question, rumbling like an endless sinister chuckle.

Stop it! She shoved dark thoughts away. "God's grace has seen us this far. He's not about to abandon us. Check your phone to see if we have cell service yet. It would help if we could let someone know where we are."

Laurel resisted the shove of the wind as she

guided the car back onto the tarmac and into their proper lane. Rudolph himself would have been grounded in this weather. A snicker rose to Laurel's lips, but she suppressed the sound. Caroline would think her mother was succumbing to blizzard madness.

"No service," Caroline said, tone dull.

"All right, then. If Estes Park is too far, we need to find other shelter. Be on the lookout for a residential driveway. A few hardy folks live out here."

"K." The single syllable sounded more upbeat.

Psychologically, in a tense situation, it helped to have a concrete goal toward a solution. Laurel schooled her breathing to remain deep and even.

"There, Mom! On my side of the road. Looks like a driveway."

Laurel took her foot off the gas and coasted the vehicle, gaze searching the swirls of white. Sure enough, a patch of gray-black widened to their right, and a small sign listing a property address number winked between snow gusts. Did she dare hope they'd found a haven? Her heart rate fluttered. But what if this was someone's vacation getaway, and no one was home? No matter. Her jaw firmed. They'd break in if necessary. This situation was life-or-death.

"Good girl." Laurel cramped the wheel to the right.

The rear tires fishtailed, but the nose of the car plowed faithfully into the turnoff. At least the driveway—which stretched on farther than she could see—was paved. The owner must be quite well off to afford the luxury.

Walls of darkness sprang up on either side of the vehicle, and the wind roar abruptly muted. Rows of sturdy pines blocked the wind's buffet, and visibility improved marginally. Still, it was hard to feel safe. The drive was too narrow, the trees loomed too close. There wasn't room to turn around in this bottleneck. They were committed to proceed until the driveway reached its destination. Long seconds passed, then minutes. Whoever owned this place must treasure seclusion in order to build so far back into the wilderness.

Finally, they emerged into a clearing, where the dense snowfall shrouded their view of a dark mass shaped like a large cabin. During split-second lulls in driving snow, a light winked at them from a window. *Thank You, God!* The sight meant warmth and shelter. Maybe even a roaring fire in the hearth?

As she stopped the vehicle, a muted cheer from Caroline drew a grin on Laurel's face. "Someone's home, sweetheart. I hope they don't mind company dropping in."

Caroline answered with a shaky chuckle.

"Are you ready to make a dash for it?" Laurel asked.

"Race you to the porch!" The teenager leaped from the vehicle.

"Whoa, there!" Laurel pressed her door open

against the thrust of the wind. "Let me find out what sort of people live here." But her words were gobbled in the roaring gale.

Icy flakes stung her cheeks, and snow drifts swallowed her legs to the calf as she struggled around the side of the car, clutching her coat hood tight beneath her chin and her purse under one arm. She battled her way up a pair of wooden steps to find Caroline knocking on the door. So much for having an opportunity to check out their potential hosts first. As if they could afford to be choosy.

The inner door swung open, and the backlit figure of a man gazed at them from behind the screen.

"Who in thunder would be out in weather like this?"

Not the friendliest greeting she'd ever encountered. She stepped closer, edging her daughter to one side, and gazed up into the man's scowl. What was familiar about him?

Their prospective host looked to be in his midthirties—not much her senior. He was of medium height and built sinewy like a marathon runner. Not classically handsome, but arresting with that square chin, rugged cheekbones and coal-black hair curling around his ears. Piercing eyes the color of fog on the ocean scanned her up and down, then flicked toward Caroline. Icicles jabbed into Laurel's marrow as recognition dawned.

David Greene—Texas oil millionaire, and accused murderer.

The money explained the paved driveway stretching at least a mile into the woods, but it didn't explain what this unconvicted killer was doing in the Rocky Mountain wilderness.

Three years ago, he'd been the chief suspect in the strangling death of his girlfriend. The man had been found, passed out from booze and drugs, beside the dead woman, but his lawyer's machinations had gotten everything incriminating removed from evidence until a grand jury concluded there wasn't enough justification to go to trial.

What does it take these days to get a conviction? said some of the friends who worked with her in their nonprofit foundation. *A sign around the louse's neck saying, I Did It?* Laurel understood the sentiment. Working daily with single parents, many of them abandoned or abused, tended to expose them to examples of wealth tipping the scales of justice until the guilty walked free and the innocent suffered. Was the Greene case another one of those?

"You'd better come in before we all freeze." The man opened the screen door.

Caroline darted forward, but Laurel grabbed her daughter's jacket sleeve. The girl shot her a wide-eyed look. Caroline probably didn't recognize their host, or she'd be tempted like her mother to run back out into the storm. Laurel glanced over her shoulder, and a wind gust shot a geyser of snow swirling from the steps onto the backs of her legs. She shivered.

On an inner groan, she released her daughter's

jacket. What choice did they have? They could freeze to death or take their chances under the roof of a possible killer.

Why today, Lord?

David assessed his unexpected guests, certain that the woman had grasped his identity in two seconds flat. She and the girl had stepped inside barely far enough for him to shut the door. The woman's wary brown gaze hadn't left him—as if she thought he might leap on them at any instant with evil intent. That's what came of his brand of notoriety, and the reaction had grown old a long time ago.

The girl seemed oblivious, gazing around the rustic luxury of the cabin with hardly a second glance for her reluctant host. In fact, her gaze seemed riveted on the baby grand piano. Was he in for an afternoon of "Chopsticks" on the ivories?

Why today of all days for drop-ins, Lord?

The repeated mental question held more than a hint of a whine. Not a worthy or wise approach toward the Almighty.

David took a deep breath. Better start over, both with God and with his guests. He could hardly send the shivering pair back into the storm, however much he wanted to be alone today—the anniversary of Alicia's death.

"Hi—uh—I'm David Greene." As if the woman didn't know. "Leave your wet shoes on the mat by the door. May I take your coats? There's a fire." He motioned toward the cozy blaze snapping in the fireplace. Now he was babbling like an imbecile. Why could he never get used to the waves of suspicion wafting from people? He cleared his throat. "You can warm your feet."

A big grin bloomed on the girl's delicate features, an immature copy of her companion's more defined face. The girl's mother or her older sister?

"Great! I'm Caroline," the teenager said as she scraped her snow-laden shoes off her feet. She tipped her hood down, revealing a thick blond ponytail, and then shrugged out of the jacket. Underneath she wore the standard teenage garb of jeans and layered shirts.

The woman responded more slowly, shedding her soggy shoes and long coat, reluctance etched in drawn brows. She wore a green print blouse and a pair of tan slacks. The outfit complimented her fair complexion and slender figure. In her stocking feet, the top of her tawny head barely reached David's chin. She clutched her coat tight to her chest, even as the girl relinquished hers to his care.

"I'm Laurel Adams, and this is my daughter, Caroline," the woman said.

A soft flush of color crept across high cheekbones as she no doubt realized that the girl had already introduced herself. At least now the relationship between the pair was clarified.

Rubbing her hands together, Caroline took off for

a spot near the hearth. The girl sank into an easy chair and extended her toes toward the fire.

"Way cool that you're out here in the middle of nowhere," she said. "I pictured Mom and me as popsicles in a ditch or pancakes over the edge of a cliff." She darted David a half smile.

He grinned back, and the tension under his breastbone eased. He could like this kid. Of course, she might not be so friendly with him when her mother informed her who he was.

A stiff smile tipped the corners of Laurel's lips. "Thank you for taking us in, Mr. Greene."

Like he had an option? But then, since she assumed him a killer, she probably thought he was fully capable of slamming the door in their faces.

Suppressing an inner sigh, David took hold of Laurel's jacket, his direct stare challenging her to release the garment. She let it go and backed away, gaze darting between her daughter and him. He headed for the coat closet next to the entrance to the kitchen. Receding footfalls said that his lovely, frightened guest had scurried for the hearth.

He hung their coats, then swiveled to find Laurel seated in a chair beside her daughter. Her focus was on him. Questions shouted from her expression. He could imagine what they might be. "Did you kill your girlfriend?" probably topped the list. Most folks couldn't bring themselves to be so blunt as to ask the question directly, but then, most people weren't snowed in with him.

"Our cell phones don't have service here," she said. "Would you have a landline so we can let people know where we are?"

An innocuous question, if a person ignored the sub-text of fear.

He shook his head. "No landline. When I come to the mountains, I'm not big on communicating with the outside world."

Her lips flattened, then she attempted another smile that only succeeded in becoming an anxious grimace. "How about internet service? We could instant message or email or—"

He shook his head. "I have a CB radio. I can give a holler to the authorities in Estes Park as to your whereabouts, and they can communicate with your husband or anyone you'd like."

"It's just Mom and me." Caroline waved a breezy hand. "Has been for a long ti—"

The pointed clearing of her mother's throat cut the girl's words short, but David got the picture. Or at least a hint. The specific reason for the absent dad/husband remained a mystery.

"You won't be going anywhere soon anyway," he said. "This storm is anticipated to last through the night, and it'll be longer than that before the roads are cleared. Why don't we take the chill off over a cup of coffee? Or cocoa or tea, if you prefer."

"Tea would be awesome." Caroline threw a grin over her shoulder. "Do you have anything fruity and spicy? Sniffing the steam jazzes my sinuses."

A chuckle spurted from David even as the girl's mother darted her daughter one of those Mom looks.

"Caroline, we can't expect our host to wait on us."

The girl's expression flattened. "But—"

"I offered, Ms. Adams," David said.

"Yeah, he offered." Caroline's infectious grin sparkled forth.

David tendered a slight smile in return. "Tea it is, then. If you're looking for something to do, help yourself to a book or a board game." He waved toward the floor-to-ceiling set of shelves built into the opposite wall.

"Thanks, Mr. Greene." The girl bounced to her feet. "I know my mom's bummed about missing her speaking gig, but we might as well make the best of being snowed in. Right?"

"You're a public speaker, Ms. Adams?"

His question jerked Laurel's focus away from her daughter, and her gaze met his. A spark lit the brown depths. "I travel quite a bit, speaking to groups about grief, loss and single parenthood."

"Yeah, and she's even got a reputation for being funny. Can you figure that?" Caroline giggled as she drifted toward the laden bookshelf.

"Really?" David raised his eyebrows.

Color rose in Laurel's face.

He swallowed a smile. Whether or not her speeches were funny, the subject matter was still serious. Raising a kid alone was no laughing matter. Not that he'd know about it firsthand, but the mere thought gave him the willies.

Laurel's chin lifted, and she rose in a fluid motion that dripped elegant dignity. David caught his breath. His mother was the only other woman he'd known to command a room so completely with a simple action. An ache throbbed deep in his chest. After all these years, he still missed Mom. Always would. This woman had his mother's air of confident grace, though an unfortunate pinch of pride stiffened her spine.

Laurel wandered toward the bookshelf in Caroline's wake. "Several years back, a few partners and I started a nonprofit organization called Single Parents Coalition. Have you heard of it?"

"Can't say that I have, but it sounds like a needed service."

"Oh, it is!" Her whole face softened and lit, and David's heart went kabump for reasons he couldn't entirely explain. Perhaps he was just responding to her passion for her vocation.

"I'll get the tea." He faded into the small but complete kitchen, and got busy at the single-cup brewer.

He shouldn't let himself be too interested in his uninvited guests. There was no point in getting friendly with these people. The cloud of suspicion over his head nullified any prospect of warmth or ease between them.

Too bad even *he* didn't know for sure what happened three years ago. He had no recollection beyond a night of partying that ended with him passing out—normal in those days.

What wasn't usual? Waking up to the cold snap of handcuffs around his wrists, the reading of rights snarled from an icy-faced detective and the chilling sight of his girlfriend—a woman he'd planned to make his fiancée—lying lifeless by his side, strangled to death with her own scarf.

Sometime during his blackout had he attacked Alicia? That was the question he'd hoped to answer during this annual time of seclusion and crying out to God to release his memories. Maybe he'd get a breakthrough this time. Even if he discovered the worst about himself, at least he would *know.* The truth would bring a form of peace. It would be a relief to own up and take his punishment.

Now he was stuck with these people invading his space and his chance for self-reflection was lost. In its place, he got the judgment of strangers. Couldn't they at least offer him the benefit of the doubt? But why should they? He didn't even know if he should offer *himself* that much grace. Yet what no one seemed to understand was that as long as suspicion of murder hung over his head, rejection and isolation ensured he was serving a life sentence in Solitary.

The tune of "Chopsticks" from the baby grand dragged David from his mulligrubs. He flashed a wry smile toward the fresh lemon he was slicing into wedges. Caroline, no doubt. He added the dish of lemon to the tea tray and headed with it toward his guests.

"Honey, you haven't asked permission to touch our host's piano."

The soft-voiced rebuke from Laurel met his ears as he entered the living room.

"It's all right," he said, taming his grin.

Caroline whirled from the piano, ponytail flipping and color in her cheeks. "I'm sorry, Mr. Greene."

"No problem." He set the tray on the small dining table in front of Laurel. "Feel free to do the honors." He motioned toward the steaming teapot and the empty cups.

If he didn't know better, he might think a smile had flickered across Laurel's face. She poured the tea with quiet dignity.

"Thank you, Mr. Greene." She handed him a cup, her gaze frank and open. "You've been very gracious to a couple of strangers bounding in on you."

David barely stopped his jaw from sagging as he accepted the offering—both the tea and the slight thaw in attitude.

"Call me David, please. When you say Mr. Greene I feel like you're talking to my father, and if you shorten it to Dave I'll think I've gone back to grade school."

"David, then. But you—" Laurel wagged a finger at her daughter "—should refer to him as Mr. Greene. It's basic respect, like the way you address your teachers at school."

"Gotcha, Mom." Caroline accepted her cup and brought it to her nose. "Mmmm. This stuff smells great! Thanks, Mr. Greene." Her enthusiasm was followed by a distinct slurp.

A chuckle escaped David's throat, and Laurel lifted her cup to hide what looked like a suspicious twitch of the lips. Small talk occupied the next minutes, but at last David set his cup down and stood.

"I can fire up that CB radio now. It might take me a few minutes to tune it in to the right frequency. I've almost never used the gadget."

Laurel rose. "Yes, please, that would be great. Let me know when I can speak to someone. In the meantime, I'd like to step outside and bring in our luggage. It would be so good to freshen up a little."

"I wouldn't feel right leaving you to go out in the storm." He moved toward the coat closet and grabbed his outdoor gear. "I'll get the bags if you give me your keys. We can do the radio after your things are inside."

"You've done enough for us, Mr. Greene. I'll handle it."

Stubborn woman. His mom had been, too, but in her the trait hadn't irritated him. "We'll do it together, then." If he could take back the bite in his tone he would.

Posture stiff, Laurel took her coat from him. He resisted the impulse to hold the garment while she shrugged into it. Under current circumstances, the common courtesy ingrained into him by his upbringing might feel like an invasion of her space. He put on his jacket, hat, boots and insulated mittens, but refrained from commenting about the wet loafers on his guest's feet.

"I'll set up a game of Scrabble while you get the bags," Caroline said.

Tugging on thin gloves, Laurel nodded at her daughter and led the way to the door. David pulled it open for her. At least he could do that much.

Snow particles stung his cheeks, and icy air washed David's face as he forged onto the porch after Laurel. He followed close on her heels as she eased down the steps. As she reached the ground, a drift swallowed her legs to the knees. He shook his head. She should have unbent enough to let him do this for her.

Frowning, he slogged after her toward the dark bulk of the car. The wind had already driven snowdrifts up to the bumpers. At last they reached the car's trunk. Laurel fished a set of keys out of her coat pocket and pressed a button. The trunk lid sprang open, blocking the wind. David gratefully inhaled a long breath free of ice particles.

Laurel's scream froze the oxygen in his chest. The car keys dropped from his guest's lax fingers. David caught the keychain, then followed the line of her gaze into the trunk. There were suitcases, all right. But something was sprawled atop them. Or rather someone. The fact that this person was no longer among the living was clear in the frozen stare and facial expression locked into an unnatural contortion.

Bitter bile stung the back of David's throat. He'd seen the body of a murder victim before—exactly three years ago to this day. At least no one could claim he'd killed *this* woman.

The same couldn't be said of his guests.

TWO

How could this be? Laurel blinked and shook her head, but the corpse draped across her luggage didn't disappear. And Laurel knew the woman. Did she ever!

How did the body of Melissa Eldon—Caroline's detested biology teacher—wind up in her car trunk? Laurel's pulse roared in her ears. How did the woman die? No noticeable injuries sprang to Laurel's attention.

And where did Ms. Eldon meet her end? Absurd to believe she crawled into the trunk of her own free will and expired. No restraints tethered the splayed body so she must have been dead before someone dumped her remains in the trunk—*after* Laurel stowed their bags last evening and *before* she and Caroline left town. The thuds and thumps from the trunk when they had nearly run off the road took on horrific significance. Nausea churned her stomach.

Think, Laurel. Think logically.

Other than herself, only Caroline would have had access to the car keys and the trunk remote control. She kept a spare set on top of the refrigerator in the kitchen. No! Laurel would never believe her daughter was responsible.

But what if the law didn't see it that way? Blackness edged her vision, and she swayed.

A firm hand caught her elbow. Gasping, she gazed up into eyes as gray and piercing as driven rain. Laurel went still. If only this man were someone she knew and trusted. Strong arms around her might never be more welcome. She pulled away and stiffened her spine.

"Do you know who this is?" he asked.

Laurel didn't answer. Her voice had lost the ability to respond. David tugged off one of his gloves, leaned into the open trunk and touched the woman's throat with a pair of fingers.

By an act of will, Laurel unlocked her lips. "Any pulse?" She already knew the answer, but she had to ask.

"Not a flicker." David straightened with a grimace. "You're out of luck on your suitcases. We'd better not disturb anything until the authorities get here."

"This is so awful! That poor woman!"

"We may as well sort out our thoughts inside where it's warm." His hand pressed gently against her shoulder. With the other hand he slammed the trunk closed on the grizzly vision. "We'll have to fire up that CB radio immediately."

"Right." The weak word was swallowed by the wind.

The journey back to the house passed in a blur. The next thing she knew, David was helping her out of her coat and urging her to remove her snow-cased shoes. Her toes tingled and stung, but nothing compared to the pins and needles in the pit of her stomach.

"I've got the game ready, Mom."

Caroline's cheerful announcement wrung Laurel's heart. How could she tell her daughter what they'd discovered outside? Laurel's gaze slid toward David, making a soundless plea for…what? Guidance? Moral support? Or was she hoping for a laugh and an assurance that their gruesome find had been a practical joke? If only!

A muscle in his jaw twitched. "You may as well tell her. The police will be involved soon enough, and there will be questions for all of us."

"Tell me what?" Caroline's brows drew together as she stood up. "Police? What's going on?"

Laurel drew in a shaky breath. "Let's have a seat on the sofa." She stepped toward her daughter, a hand extended.

Caroline backed away. "Stop it! You're scaring me."

"Listen to your mom, young lady," David said.

"This is too important for you to do anything but tune in with both ears."

The teenager gaped, gaze cutting toward their host.

"Please," Laurel said.

Something deflated on the inside of Caroline, and she shuffled to the sofa and plopped down. Laurel perched beside her daughter.

"There is no gentle way to break this news." If only her whisper-soft tone could perform the impossible anyway. "We—uh, Mr. Greene and I—made a shocking discovery." Her hands fisted around the fabric of her pants legs. "Your teacher—" She stopped and cleared her throat. "Your biology teacher is dead."

Caroline gaped. "That's terrible! How did you find out— Ohhhh!" Her expression lightened. "You must have gotten cell service out there and someone called you. Did you tell them where we are?"

"No, honey. No one called me. I know she's dead because I saw her with my own eyes." Laurel brushed her fingertips against her daughter's cheek. "Your teacher's body was lying across our luggage."

Caroline's face went red and then drained stark white.

"Yes, it's a terrible thing, sweetheart. Even if you didn't like Ms. Eldon, you'd never wish something like this to happen to her."

"What's going on? How did she die?" Caroline's

eyes pleaded with her mother to provide answers that would make sense of the incomprehensible.

Laurel spread her hands. "We're mystified. I didn't see any marks on the body, did you?"

She looked toward David. He shook his head. At least she wasn't so rattled she'd overlooked something obvious.

"How did she get into our car?" Caroline burst out. "I don't understand."

"None of us do." David's voice rang strong. "That's for law enforcement to figure out. I'd better go raise them on the radio."

"This is for real?" Caroline's voice went shrill.

Laurel nodded. "I'm afraid so, sweetie." If she looked half as horrified as her daughter, they were truly a miserable pair.

"Oh, Mo-o-om!"

Caroline threw herself into Laurel's arms. If only she could absorb some of the shock for her little girl, but there was more than enough of that to go around.

Over her daughter's shoulder, she glimpsed David's expression as he turned away from them and left the room. Compassion? Yes, a strong dose of that. Confusion? Who could blame him? Suspicion? No, surely not!

But why not? He didn't know them any better than they knew him, and she had been quick enough to draw conclusions about him the moment she recognized him. What irony for the shoe to suddenly find itself on the other foot! She didn't like it, but what David Greene thought was the least of their worries. They had a reprieve until the storm abated and the authorities arrived, but then she and her daughter would find themselves the focus of a murder investigation.

She could almost feel sympathy for what David had gone through. Almost. He could well be guilty, but at least she knew her own innocence and Caroline's—didn't she?

Laurel gazed into the teenager's tear-wet face. She wiped at the tears with her thumbs. Caroline might be going through a rough patch emotionally, but she'd seen no signs of potential to do this kind of harm. Deep down, her girl was still her sweet girl.

"It'll be all right, honey."

"You always tell me that."

"Haven't things always worked out?"

"They didn't work out so well for Ms. Eldon."

"I'm sorry for what happened to your teacher, but she's not my main concern. You are. Always and forever."

The ghost of a smile trembled forth. "That's sappy, Mom, but right now, I don't care. What are the cops going to say? They're going to think we killed her, aren't they."

The last sentence was more of a statement than a question. Laurel couldn't fault her daughter's intelligence. "I assume we'll be questioned, and they'll have to investigate us, but we're innocent. They'll discover that soon enough."

"Ri-i-ight! Like they exonerated Mr. Greene."

Laurel's jaw dropped. "You know who he is?"

Caroline rolled her eyes. "Sure. I was in grade school when all that stuff happened, but I don't live in a bubble. We talked about the weird case last year in our Social Studies unit on criminal justice. Even watched a recorded news segment. I have to say, Mr. Greene looks a lot cuter now than he did when he was being dogged by reporters."

"I would never have guessed you recognized him," Laurel said. "You didn't act nervous to meet him."

"I'll let you hog the Oscar for uptight performance. I just reminded myself straight off that there must be a reason why the guy wasn't indicted." Caroline lifted a forestalling hand. "I know. I know. Bad people get away with things all the time. But Mr. Greene seems like a good guy. You have to admit that sometimes good people get accused of bad things."

Laurel spurted a chuckle. "I think you've overheard too many of my phone conversations with colleagues from work. But please remember, sweetheart, that I'm a mama bear dedicated to protecting you. I've also had a little more life experience, so pardon me for being skeptical about charming exteriors."

Caroline leaned close. "You know what I think?"

"Hmm. Something about the tone of that question makes me wonder if I want to hear it."

"I think you can handle charming without wigging out, but rich *and* charming pushes all your buttons. Throw in a little suspicion of violent behavior, and the guy is presumed guilty until proven innocent."

The air stalled in Laurel's lungs. What would Caroline know about the terrors of Laurel's brief marriage to her father? She'd barely been three years old when he ditched them for a more compliant wife. Good riddance, as far as she was concerned. But since then, for Caroline's sake, Laurel had been careful to keep any mention of the man brief and honest, but as kind as possible. Well, at least not overly hostile. Had Caroline been reading between the lines all these years?

The teenager clapped her hands and laughed more heartily than Laurel had heard her in months. "You should see your face, Mom. The psychologist's daughter strikes again!"

The sound of footfalls entering the room stopped the rebuttal on Laurel's tongue. Caroline's head turned in unison with hers toward their host.

David regarded them soberly. "The sheriff and the coroner will be here as soon as the storm lets up."

The smile melted from Caroline's face, and Laurel shivered as if he had dashed her with a bucket of snow. For Melissa Eldon the worst had already happened. For her and Caroline, the worst might be about to begin.

David ripped at the bunch of romaine lettuce as if he could rend truth out of it by force. Refusing assistance from his guests, he'd retired to the kitchen to prepare a supper no one might have an appetite to eat—and to gather his thoughts. He'd left mother and daughter in the main room playing a listless game of Scrabble.

How legit were those two? If he'd ever seen pure horror on anyone's face, he saw it on Laurel's when they uncovered the dead woman in her trunk. After they came inside, Caroline's stunned reaction was as believable as her mother's. Then he left the room for a few minutes to place that radio call and came back to find them laughing—well, Caroline anyway. Laurel's expression had been confounded as a coyote staring down a rabbit hole.

Were these a pair of stellar actors, or were they as innocent as they seemed? Laurel hadn't done well at hiding her feelings from the moment he opened his front door to them, so he'd be surprised if she was that good at pretending. On the other hand, from what he'd overheard of their discussion about him, Caroline had also recognized his face and hadn't batted an eyelash. If she easily masked surprise, could she fake it, as well?

He attacked a tomato with a knife.

His brief observation of the body, clad in button-down blouse and sleek pants, revealed Ms. Eldon as tall, blonde, full-figured and leggy. Caroline was a snip of a girl. The picture of her lugging that body into the garage from wherever and lifting the corpse into the trunk simply did not compute.

David's knife halted halfway through a down-stroke into the meat of the tomato.

Unless little Caroline had an accomplice—like her too-attractive-for-his-own-good mother. They were both petite, but together they could have managed it.

Maybe he was on to something. Laurel *had* protested him joining her to collect the luggage. Maybe they were planning to ditch the corpse down one of the ravines along the route, but the snowstorm scuttled their best-laid intentions.

But then he came back to that look on Laurel's face as she stared into the trunk. He couldn't quite buy a put-on when the response was so spontaneous. Besides, if she knew the body was there, she could have been more forceful in her refusal of his help. Why did Laurel even bring up the luggage if the mention could lead to discovery of her grizzly secret? If she was that desperate to freshen up, she could have sneaked out there while he was warming up the radio and been back in with the bags before he knew she'd gone.

Then there was Caroline's cheerful announcement that she'd set up the game. No trace of anxiety and no attempt to stop them from retrieving the bags.

David began giving the salad the tossing of its life.

Could his unexpected guests be setting *him* up for some reason? The pieces didn't fit that scenario either. He didn't see how they could have planned for a snowstorm to dump them on his doorstep. Plus, he'd never met the dead woman, though there was something about her...His brows drew together. What had he glimpsed out there that gave him this feeling he needed to take another look?

He shrugged off the thought with a roll of the shoulders. He didn't know the woman. Never seen her before in his life, and he wasn't going to meddle with a crime scene. Period.

But his guests knew the dead woman, and it seemed that Caroline had cordially disliked her. That was a tick mark against the teenager, but he'd had plenty of teachers during his school career that he'd wanted to ship to Timbuktu in a packing crate. Of course, he never would have followed through with his desires, any more than Caroline's feelings about her teacher meant she'd killed the woman. Surely, the police investigators would realize that much.

Not that he had much faith in cops giving anyone the benefit of the doubt. Come to think of it, he didn't have much confidence that they'd solve the murder. Look how they'd done on his case. Lots of crimes never came to closure and left people in a limbo of pain and distrust.

David stopped tossing the salad and leaned against the counter. There was his answer. He wanted people to treat him as though he was innocent until he was proven guilty. Shouldn't he do the same for Laurel and Caroline?

"Something smells wonderful." Laurel leaned a shoulder against the kitchen door frame.

David offered her a smile, but she stared back at him as if she'd never seen one before. She was still dazed, and he couldn't blame her. He stirred the sauce bubbling on the stove.

"If you and Caroline want to set the table, we can eat in about ten or fifteen minutes."

Laurel called her daughter, and they headed to the glass-fronted cupboards that held plates and glasses.

"Wow!" the teenager said. "This kitchen's got about every technogadget on the planet."

David wrinkled his nose. "I know. It looks more like the kitchen of a five-star restaurant than a cabin in the woods. I like to cook, but the prior owner was something of a gourmand. I was told that he sometimes brought his private chef with him. I prefer doing things the old-fashioned way." He motioned toward the paring knife and cutting board.

"Which reminds me," he continued, "I'll move into the chef's bedroom tonight, and you two can have the larger bed in my room."

"You don't have to do that, Mr. Greene." Laurel said.

"Not doing it because I have to…and it's David. Remember?"

Their gazes locked. Laurel clutched a short stack of plates to her chest. Her eyes searched his. Would she be able to see that he meant her well? That he was not a threat to her safety, and that he wasn't going to judge her?

She gave a brief nod. "Thank you, then."

"Don't thank me too much." He chuckled as she headed for the sitting room with the plates, Caroline in her wake, toting fistfuls of silverware. "I'm going to make you change the sheets yourself. You'll find a stack of them in the hall closet. Take your pick."

Laurel glanced over her shoulder, a corner of her mouth quirked upward. "I think we can handle that."

Soon they sat down in front of steaming beef stroganoff, tossed salad and biscuits with honey butter.

"What an awesome feast!" Caroline eyed the serving dishes.

"I wish I had more of an appetite." Laurel's words came out softly.

Enthusiasm faded from Caroline's face, and her gaze fell to her empty plate.

"I'm sorry, honey. I shouldn't have said that." Laurel covered her daughter's hand with hers. "You enjoy this meal, and I'll do my best to follow your lead. It does smell wonderful." Her gaze cut to David and then back toward her daughter. "We can't allow ourselves to feel guilty for living."

Caroline gazed at David. "You can tell she's got a master's degree in psychology, right?"

David folded his hands. "You can be thankful for and take pride in an intelligent and well-educated mother." Did he detect a smidgeon of gratitude in Laurel's eyes?

"Um, yeah." Caroline's nose wrinkled the barest degree.

"You can tell my daughter has never looked at the matter that way before." Laurel's statement was directed toward David but her attention was fixed on her daughter. Their stares dueled.

"Feel free to dig in." David delivered the invitation, then closed his eyes and bowed his head to say a soundless grace.

He didn't believe in making them uncomfortable by pushing his faith on them. He was more the live-it-and-trust-they-see-something-they-want sort of soul winner.

Lord, I'm trying but I could use a little help. There's some serious healing to be done between these two, not to mention a crime to solve. Of course, You know that. I'm a bucket of problems with my own crime to solve, so if You'd bring them across the path of someone who can help them sort things out, I'd be grateful... Oh, and thank You for this food. Amen.

Silence rang in his ears. Weren't the ladies going

to eat? He opened his eyes a sliver, then widened them all the way. His guests sat with heads bowed over their plates. Laurel's lips moved without sound. Caroline's head came up, and a smile flickered at him as she reached for the stroganoff. Her mother's gaze lifted slowly, no smile, but she helped herself to the mixed green salad.

Were these two fellow Christians? Maybe his after supper plans would help clarify the matter. His gaze traveled to the baby grand as he reached for the biscuits.

"Caroline, I noticed you play the piano."

"A little bit," she said. "I've only had a couple years of lessons."

"Do you like playing?"

The girl pursed her lips. "I love music. I'm just not sure if I can play well enough to make it worth the cost of the lessons."

"Honey, cut yourself some slack," Laurel said. "You've come a long way, but you can hardly expect to be a professional yet. Mastering an instrument takes time and effort."

"More effort than I've been putting in, you mean."

"I didn't say—"

"Let's tickle a few ivories after supper," David put in quickly. "Just for fun. No *Beethoven's Fifth Symphony* or anything. But first—" he wagged his fork at Caroline "—you and your mom put the dishes in the dishwasher. Cleaning up is the part of cooking

I *don't* like." He waggled his eyebrows, and Caroline giggled.

"You're on, Mr. Greene. I'd do dishes every night to eat like this. Mom tries, but cooking isn't her thing. It's lucky that I like bake-at-home pizza, sub sandwich delivery and Chinese takeout." She gave a brief lift of her shoulders, laughed and then stuffed a bite of stroganoff into her mouth. Her eyes drifted closed as she chewed, and a soft hum purred from her throat.

David grinned and then the smile faded as Laurel laid her fork aside and dabbed at her mouth with a napkin. Had Caroline's offhand remark about her mom's cooking brought that expression to her face as if she'd tasted something nasty? The sorrow that darkened those honey-rich eyes seemed deeper than a simple lack of culinary skills might cause. There were undercurrents here that he didn't understand and wasn't sure he wanted to navigate.

Small talk continued over the meal. David's effort to remain upbeat flagged as shadows settled over his guest's expressions. Clearing up time couldn't come fast enough. While Laurel and Caroline saw to the dishes, David tended the blaze in the fireplace.

"Are you up for 'Chopsticks' then?" He waved a hand toward the piano.

Caroline backed away a step. "Seriously?"

"Go for it. I promise you it will turn out better than you think. I'll help you."

"You play?"

He grinned. "I didn't truck this piano up here just to look at it."

Caroline's cheeks pinked but she spurted a brief chuckle. "I suppose not." She took a seat on the polished mahogany bench and placed her fingers on the keyboard.

Notes emerged hesitantly and then picked up speed. About the time Caroline hit a good cadence David slid onto the bench beside her and began to play a high counterpoint melody. She shot him a startled glance and stumbled over a few notes, then resumed her tune in earnest.

Laurel, who had come to stand to one side of the piano, rewarded him with a smile and a nod. David almost botched his next note.

The woman was lovely. Not in an exotic way—a hothouse flower like Alicia had been. Or in a delicate and fleeting sort of way like a rose. But with the graceful purity of the calla lily. He should know. On his Texas ranch, he grew plots of the stunning flowers that had been his mother's favorite. But now he was likely doomed to see another face in his mind's eye whenever he tended his plants.

Get a grip, dude. He turned his attention on Caroline. "What else do you know?"

"Not much, but here goes." Caroline moved into a rousing rendition of "Jingle Bells."

Chuckling, David switched positions to her other side and began a bass note accompaniment. The girl's sunny grin turned his insides to mush. He'd be nothing but pleased if he could be 100 percent certain the two of them had nothing to do with the demise of the woman in their car trunk.

"That's it. I'm done." Caroline slid off the bench. "Now let's hear what you can do."

"Yes, please." Laurel seconded the invitation. "Though that was really nice, honey. I'm proud of you." She slid an arm around her daughter, and Caroline didn't pull away.

"You asked for it." David moved to the center of the bench.

The keys were cool velvet beneath his fingertips. If anything other than gardening had saved his sanity these past few years, it was his music—another legacy from his mother. He transitioned into an airy rendition of "My Favorite Things" and then toned it down with *Für Elise*.

"Hey, I recognize that one," Caroline said. "It's Beethoven. I'll bet you *could* play his *Fifth Symphony,* no problem."

"I can, but I'm not going to. How about this one?" He began "Morning Has Broken." A few chords into the song a clear, strong voice took up the words. A heartbeat later, a more youthful voice joined Laurel's.

"You two can sing." David smiled big. "This is going to be fun."

Time drifted as they moved from one familiar favorite to the next—a few pop songs to please the teenager, but mostly praise choruses or old-fashioned hymns. At last, David pulled his hands from the keyboard and let out a slow breath. His guests echoed the soft sigh. Calm and peace enveloped the room. Rare commodities, especially under current circumstances.

"I think," Laurel said quietly, "this would be a good note on which to say good-night." She nudged her daughter. "Good night, David. And thank you."

The gentle light in Laurel's eyes played a tune on David's insides.

"Thanks, Mr. Greene," Caroline said as she allowed herself to be guided away.

The mild flurry of them changing the bedding and him lending them T-shirts and drawstring bottoms for sleepwear did little to disrupt the precious serenity.

"Your peace in the midst of trouble is such a gift, God," David said as he pulled the covers over himself in the cook's bed.

The mattress was harder than he liked and the pillow too thin, but he wasn't about to complain. To God or to himself. He closed his eyes and let his thoughts drift.

He'd come up to the mountains to be alone and seek the truth. That plan had taken a major detour. Now, he might believe the disruption was a blessing in disguise—except murder had once again invaded his life.

No, he didn't want to go there. He needed to

hang on for dear life to the evening's calm. But his thoughts had a mind of their own.

A stark vision formed in his head. Pale hair cascaded across shiny black luggage. Blue eyes and red lips frozen open. The blouse twisted away from one shoulder. An etched mark beneath the bare collarbone. A tattoo!

David lunged upright in bed, heart catching in his throat. The whole tattoo hadn't been visible—maybe half. The rest remained covered by the blouse. He'd only idly noticed it, as he'd been absorbed with the shock of the discovery and the futile search for a pulse. His hand had nearly brushed the telltale mark.

No wonder he'd had this feeling he needed to take another look at the body. His subconscious had registered what his consciousness had overlooked. He'd known one other woman with a similar tattoo in an identical spot. That woman was also dead, and he was suspected of killing her.

THREE

Lying flat in the cushy bed, Laurel stared into the dark. The wind wailed around the corner of the cabin, raging against denied entrance. No wonder people's minds could slip when trapped in a storm. The constant drone tweaked every nerve.

If she could relax, maybe she could sleep. Laurel rolled over onto her side. She'd dozed off for a while after they'd first turned in, but the reprieve from consciousness had been short-lived. No way would she get another wink tonight, despite the luxury of silken sheets and a down-filled pillow,

That poor woman—murdered! What of Ms. Eldon's family—her parents? As a mother, Laurel could imagine the pain of learning about the loss of a daughter to foul play. How awful for them! What would she do if she lost Caroline?

Caroline.

The name sighed through Laurel's thoughts. The friction between them continued and had perhaps escalated. Why had Caroline never told her that she craved home-cooked meals—or that anything her mother made might be better off in the trash?

So cooking wasn't Laurel's strong suit. She'd be the first to admit it, and the shortcoming hadn't bothered her much. Until now. Caroline's casual remark, comparing her abilities to those of a total stranger, had cut to the quick. Why had Caroline bonded with this suspected murderer with such ease when she could hardly offer her mother a civil word?

Laurel could resent David for his charming ways that seemed to have mesmerized her daughter, but surely she wasn't that petty. The pleasant atmosphere he'd gone out of his way to provide deserved high marks. His efforts went beyond simply being charming. Given his apparent prayer before the meal and his song repertoire, he might even be a fellow believer in Christ. Why did that idea dismay her rather than comfort her? Maybe because Christ-follower and murderer were two roles that didn't reconcile.

What *was* she to believe about this man? Perhaps the best she could do was to strive to withhold judgment. His guilt or innocence wasn't her concern, after all. She had more pressing worries.

When the sheriff arrived, what was going to happen to Caroline and her? How could she protect her daughter?

God, have mercy!

If that was the best prayer she could offer, she was a pitiful specimen. She couldn't seem to muster so much as a mustard seed of faith to mix with pleas for help and guidance. How long had she been so dry spiritually?

Too long. The answer echoed in her mind.

From the tossing and turning on the other side of the bed, apparently Caroline wasn't sleeping either. In fact, the girl seemed to be doing her best to maintain the greatest distance possible from her mother. Not a difficult task in this king-size bed.

"Do you believe I might have done it?"

The whispered question electrified the darkness.

"Done what?"

"You know."

Laurel's heart wept. "Why would you ask such a thing, honey?"

"You answered my question with a question. I guess that gives me my answer."

"No, sweetheart. I never suspected you for a minute."

Caroline snorted. "Yeah, but I'll bet you had to analyze the situation for at least fifty-nine seconds before you made up your mind what you were going to believe. You never accept anyone or anything at face value."

Laurel caught her breath. Was this how Caroline viewed her mother's carefully cultivated caution and prudence? How could Laurel correct that perception? The solution to that problem would have to wait. Caroline needed reassurance right now.

"I *know* you, baby girl. There's nothing in you capable of doing...whatever was done to Ms. Eldon."

Her daughter sighed. "But you think I'm manifesting deep-seated abandonment issues." Caroline bracketed the last half of her sentence in a tone that mimicked Laurel's dictation voice following a professional counseling session.

The accusing words jabbed at Laurel, but she firmed her insides. "We had this discussion in the car. Are you saying there's no possibility that Emily's leaving hasn't opened up some emotional scar tissue that you didn't realize was there?"

"I don't know, Mom." The words emerged as a miserable whine. "I'm going to try to get some sleep." The girl rolled over, presenting her back to her mother.

Laurel swallowed a foul lump in her throat. What fine-sounding psychobabble had she spouted? Such statements sounded wise and understanding during her public talks, but in the wee hours of the morning in this demented situation, they fell flat. Had her mission and ministry amounted to no more than empty air?

A noise grabbed Laurel's attention. Was that the front door closing? She hadn't heard their host leave his bedroom up the hall from theirs. The barest waft of chilly air moved through the room, and the hairs on her arms stood to attention.

David or an intruder? How would the latter be

possible in the middle of the night in this storm? Laurel sat up.

"Do you hear someone in the living room?"

Caroline yawned but didn't stir. "Must be Mr. Greene. He padded past here a little while ago. Probably can't sleep either."

"Oh." Lame, but Laurel had no better response to offer. She hadn't heard the earlier movement, no doubt because she'd been so lost in fretting that other sounds hadn't penetrated.

"I think I'll get a glass of water."

"K."

Laurel slipped from between the sheets and stood on the scatter rug by the bed. She took a step onto the hardwood floor and quickly retreated onto the rug. The cabin definitely didn't have heated floors. Probably not even a basement, just a crawlspace beneath. Thankfully, electric baseboard heat kept the air in each room tolerably warm. She sucked in a breath and tiptoed quickly up the hall and into the carpeted living area.

The glow from the dying embers in the fireplace revealed that the room was vacant. Had David returned to his bed? How would that be possible? He would have had to walk past her to get back to his end of the hall. She looked toward the front door. His boots were missing. Why would he have gone out into the storm in the middle of the night?

Laurel went to the front window, parted the curtains and peered out. A ghostly wall of white shimmered in the darkness and hid any form or movement. Where was David Greene? Her heart thudded against her ribs as her misspent youth of watching horror movies played gruesome possibilities through her mind. Shivering, she drew back from the window.

"Don't be silly," she whispered aloud. But her arms slid around her frame in a tight hug.

What if David's midnight mission had something to do with the murder? Was he out there satisfying morbid curiosity and messing with things he shouldn't? Should she throw on her shoes and outerwear and go after him? *Yeah, right!* as her daughter might say. She'd get two steps away from the porch and be unable to find either the cabin or her car.

She should go get a bottle of water. Her mouth had gone dry as the last pan of brownies she'd tried to bake. But while she was in the kitchen she could acquire a weapon—a knife, a meat mallet—whatever it took to stand between any threat and her daughter. If she was indulging morbid night fancies, she'd be happy to feel foolish in the morning with a defensive weapon under her pillow rather than ignore her inner alarms. She'd ignored those alarms more than once while married to Caroline's father and lived to regret it.

In fact, she was lucky she'd lived.

Laurel headed for the refrigerator. The bottoms of her feet registered the chill as she left the carpet for the kitchen tile. She flipped on the light rather than risk adding a stubbed toe to cold feet. The kitchen was as tidy as they'd left it. Their host's excuse for nighttime prowling wasn't the quest for a snack.

Her gaze scanned the countertops and landed on a wood block bristling with knife handles. Weapons search over. Her hand closed around the handle of the largest one, but a sound at the front door froze her in place.

"Brrr!" someone muttered and feet stomped the floor. David? Probably. But she couldn't be certain. And even if it was David, did that mean she was safe?

What legitimate purpose could he have for sneaking outside this time of night? She slid the knife from its housing and turned to face their host. If he was a threat, she was ready.

Her knees shook, but she firmed her spine as a parka-clad figure filled the kitchen doorway, face shrouded in a fur-lined hood. Her gaze fell to the items he carried, and her insides went limp.

Clutching a load of firewood in the crook of one arm and a flashlight in the other hand, David took in the stark fear staring at him from the pallor of Laurel's face. Then he dropped his gaze to the knife in her fist. His jaw clenched. So his efforts to re-assure his guests this evening hadn't reduced his threat level in her mind.

"Looking for a snack?" he said, forcing his tone as near to natural as he could muster. "There's some brick cheese in the fridge that might need slicing, but I don't think you'll need the butcher knife."

Her head snapped back as if his words had slapped her. "No—um— No, of course not. I was just…" She lowered the knife to her side, at a loss to finish her sentence.

"Let me put this wood down by the fireplace, and I'll help make sandwiches. I could use one, too… and a cup of cocoa. It's freezing out there, and big daddy storm hasn't let up any."

"Sounds fine." She nodded. "I'll get started on the cocoa." She moved to the single cup brewer and plucked a K-Cup from the carousel next to it.

David plodded to the fireplace. He knelt and dumped the load of stubby logs into the box on the hearth. He should be angry with her. Furious even. Or at least offended, but the best he could muster was this deep sadness that weighted the pit of his stomach.

He rose and shed his parka, then tossed it onto one of the pair of easy chairs with more force than necessary. Maybe he *was* a little angry. He exchanged his boots for the house slippers he'd left on the rug by the door and rejoined his guest in the kitchen.

Laurel was standing at the brewer flamingo-style with one foot on the tile and the other pressed against the navy knit of her sweatpants. Unexpectedly, his heart warmed. Was he that starved for domesticity that the sight of a female at the homey chore turned him sappy? The two of them were on little more than speaking terms. Still, the tawny, sleep-tousled hair brushing her shoulders only added to her appeal.

She turned toward him with a pair of steaming mugs in her hands, and he mustered a smile. "Why don't you take those into the living room, and I'll make the sandwiches. Your bare feet must be chilled to the bone."

Gaze averted, color high on her cheeks, she nodded and hustled from the room. Sighing, David dug cold cuts and cheese from the refrigerator. A few minutes later, he laid a plate beside her cocoa on a side table. She'd left the living room light off, but the glow from the kitchen conspired with the fireplace embers to outline her form curled up on the easy chair with her feet under her.

"Here." He stripped the throw blanket from the back of the couch and laid it across her lap. No word of thanks or eye contact acknowledged his courtesy. What was with this woman? Either she was still petrified of him or her mind was consumed with what lay outside in the trunk of her car. Or maybe a healthy dollop of both. Good thing she had no idea what he'd really been doing outside.

"I'll stoke the fire," he said.

A jingle stopped him in the act of turning away. He swiveled toward her. A set of car keys dangled from her fingers.

"I found these on the floor near your parka."

"Really?"

"They must have fallen out of your pocket."

"I—I suppose so."

"What were you doing with them?" Even in the twilight, her gaze skewered him. "And how did you get them?"

Heart thumping, he went to the hearth, knelt and began positioning logs in the fireplace. Better if he answered this with his back to her. His face was likely to give him away. "You dropped them. Remember?"

"Dropped them! I don't—" Her words halted. "Oh, yes," she said, tone subdued. "When we found the— When we went outside to get the luggage."

"That's right." With the poker, David prodded the fresh logs into position on the embers. "Guess I must have stuck them into my pocket after I caught them in midair."

"So your excursion into the storm had nothing to do with the keys that happened to be in your pocket. You went outside for more wood?"

David swallowed against a dry throat. "There's a box on the porch."

"We don't need the fire in the fireplace for heat in the house."

"True, but a little blaze is nice if you can't sleep and want to toast your toes and sip cocoa."

He inserted bits of tinder into the smoldering ashes, and flames began to flicker. If only he could be so successful in calming his guest's suspicions.

"I can't argue with that statement." A soft slurp followed her words.

David rose and turned to find Laurel standing with her keys in one hand and her mug in the other. The blanket had slid onto the floor and lay crumpled at her feet.

"I'll take this to bed with me." She raised the mug. "Thanks for making the snack, but I guess I really don't feel like eating. Enjoy your cozy fire."

The flatly spoken words hung in the air as her graceful stride carried her from the room. David's gaze followed her retreat—empty protests, explanations, reassurances locked behind his tongue.

Good thing he'd never aspired to an acting career. He stunk at it. Laurel's body language communicated that she didn't believe he'd told her the truth. Well, he had; just not the whole truth. Before he grabbed the wood, he went out to her car first and verified his glimpse of that tattoo on the body. The tat was there, all right. His memory hadn't played him false.

He picked up the blanket and settled onto the sofa next to his sandwich and cocoa. Frowning, he sipped at his hot beverage, then ran stiff fingers through his hair. The thick mop needed cutting, but a trim hadn't seemed important before he went on a solo retreat to the mountains. Who could have predicted so many complications to a simple plan?

David set his mug on a side table, leaned forward—elbows on his knees—and gazed into the blossoming fire. What was the meaning behind the nearly identical tattoos on jet-setting Alicia and this middle school biology teacher? Was there a real connection between the dead women, or were the tattoos a coincidence? The questions seared his mind, demanding answers. Where did he start looking for them?

Maybe he should hire another private investigator. This would be his fourth. The notion left a sour taste in his mouth. He'd had nothing but empty promises and bills from every P.I. he'd hired to look into Alicia's murder. Call him paranoid, but he'd had the sense that even the P.I.s on his payroll had figured him as the culprit. Had they looked very hard to find another explanation? Why would they take him seriously this time? No, he wasn't going to go that route again.

He could point out the similar tattoos to the police once they arrived and let *them* follow the lead. His insides shriveled. What was he thinking? Major bad idea. If the police caught wind of the tattoo connection on another dead body in his vicinity, they were as likely to try to pin this second murder on him as to look further for answers.

Before he went to the cops with this similarity between the murder victims, he needed to have some idea how the tattoos might point to a different culprit. He knew he hadn't killed the high school teacher, so if the murders were connected, then this could be proof that he hadn't killed Alicia either. He sat up stiff.

Did he dare hope the tats signaled his innocence? Or was he setting himself up for bitter disappointment? At this point, there was no way to tell. He'd have to uncover the significance of the ink markings for himself before he could trust this knowledge to anyone—even the woman who owned the car where the teacher's body was stowed.

For all he knew, Laurel or her daughter had a hand in the teacher's death or knew something about it. Either they were innocent victims of a frame-up, or they were devious and culpable. Either way, innocent or diabolical, he needed to keep an eye on those two until the tattoo business was explained.

FOUR

An unusual noise roused Laurel. Rather, the lack of noise. No wind howl! The cabin lay in blessed stillness. She'd been certain she wouldn't sleep, but she'd actually dozed off after that disturbing encounter with their host.

The man confounded her. At times, he was gallantry personified. But she'd learned the hard way to be wary of too nice exteriors. On the other hand, he could be moody and sharp. His first words to them when they appeared on his doorstep proven that much. Also, he had been angry at her mistrust of him when she'd clutched that knife last night. She'd seen it in his eyes and had felt about two inches high. How many times had she promised herself not to overreact to situations where she had to be alone with a male—especially a man of means and power—who was an unknown quantity? Psychologist, heal thyself! Easier said than done.

When she'd gone from the kitchen to the living room last night, she'd had good intentions to apologize for her defensive behavior as soon as he came in with the sandwiches…then she'd found her car keys on the floor by his parka. Maybe she hadn't fooled him, but he hadn't fooled her either with that song and dance about only going out to fetch wood from the porch.

Had he done something out there that could further incriminate her or Caroline? Had he tampered with the evidence in some way? Those questions had no answers. At least not yet.

David Greene harbored secrets. The man had motives for doing things that she didn't understand and dared not trust. He was gifted, and charismatic and attractive. Even without his suspicious past, all of that would have been enough to make her wary. Add the wherewithal for him to carry out any purpose he planned, and her peace of mind was blown out of the water.

On the other side of the bed, Caroline's breaths came deep and even. How long would her daughter be allowed to enjoy sleep? The sheriff had said they would be out as soon as the storm subsided.

Laurel sat up on her elbow. The first blush of predawn peeked around the edges of the blinds on the bedroom window. She grabbed her wristwatch from the side table. The lit face stared back at her. A little after five.

As if the thought conjured company, a sound rumbled from outside—a full-throated engine. Faint and distant, but drawing closer.

She laid a hand on her daughter's shoulder. "Caroline, I'm sorry, honey, but I think we should get up and get dressed. I suspect the authorities are about to arrive."

The girl groaned and lifted her head from the pillow. "Yeah, I know, Mom. I hear it, too."

Her tone was subdued. Sad like only a teenager can be. But in this situation, Caroline had more reason than most. Laurel restrained the impulse to gather her daughter close. No time. Quite likely her gesture would be rejected anyway.

Laurel got up and switched on a light, then they scrambled into their clothes. Sounds came from David's room. He must have heard the rumble, too. Laurel left the bedroom, trailed by Caroline. David stepped into the hallway at the same moment, and Laurel pulled up short. Caroline bumped into her from behind, and a soft *ooph* left their lips in unison.

Clad in sweatpants and a T-shirt that fit nicely over his athletic frame, David offered a rueful half smile that gleamed white in a darkly attractive halo of five o'clock shadow. Five in the morning, that is.

"Sorry about that." He ran fingers through the dishevelment of his bedhead. "Here they come; ready or not."

The rumble outside grew to a roar, then abruptly the engine noise powered down to a loud purr. Laurel's heart tap-danced against her ribs.

"Mo-o-om! It's a snowplow, and there are cop cars behind it." The call came from the living room.

Laurel tore her gaze from David's and hurried up the hall. She found Caroline standing at the front window, holding the curtains apart. Laurel stepped up behind her.

Headlights and red-and-blue strobes sliced away the paling gloom outside the window, leaving the cabin exposed. Defenseless. Maybe a dozen feet away sat her car, a modest four-door with snow piled to the tops of its hubcaps. Who would guess the ordinary vehicle was someone's coffin? The car was surrounded by a snowplow, two sheriff's units and an ambulance-style vehicle. The ME's transportation?

"Don't mention your personal feelings about Ms. Eldon unless they ask," Laurel said softly over her daughter's shoulder.

"I know, Mom. I'm not stupid." The girl snorted, and Laurel bit back a sigh.

A tall, stocky man emerged from one of the law enforcement vehicles and waded toward the front door. The star on his jacket glinted as he passed a set of headlights. A man and a woman climbed out of a second sheriff's vehicle and followed their leader.

Laurel tugged Caroline away from the window, and the teenager didn't balk. Heavy footfalls reverberated on the porch steps, and Laurel's heart rate kicked into a gallop. Caroline whimpered. Laurel drew her close and pressed her lips to a spot beside

Caroline's ear. When had her daughter grown nearly as tall as her?

A loud rap sounded at the front door. She looked toward David, and he offered a grave nod as he went to answer it. Laurel took in a deep breath while Caroline cowered closer. Frigid air slapped their faces as the door opened, followed by the entrance of the law enforcement trio. They stomped white-coated feet on the entry rug and stared around the cozy area. Laurel steeled herself not to flinch beneath their assessing looks.

"Sheriff Nate O'Dell here," the lead man said, "and these are my deputies, Aaron Teel and Carly Mackin." The sheriff's flat gaze zeroed in on David. "You'd be Greene then? The one who radioed?"

"That'd be me." David lifted a hand.

The sheriff grunted while the deputies scanned him up and down as if he were an intriguing but loathsome specimen. Sympathy for David rippled through Laurel. It couldn't be fun going through life dealing with those looks. Maybe he deserved them, but maybe not. Would she and Caroline soon be the object of such stares?

"Show me the body in the trunk," the sheriff said. "An EMT and the medical examiner are waiting in the ambulance to get started on the remains. My deputies will stay here and take statements." His gaze found Laurel. "You are?"

"Laurel Adams from Denver," her voice rasped through a dry throat. She swallowed her last drop of saliva. "This is my daughter, Caroline." At least her second sentence came out in a normal tone.

The sheriff turned toward his deputies. "Aaron, you speak to Ms. Adams here, and Carly, you can take the daughter in the other room." He stepped toward the door.

"Excuse me." Laurel's tone emerged a great deal stronger than she felt, but this was her daughter at stake. "Caroline is underage, and I am her mother—her only parent. She will speak to no one outside of my presence. Besides, she had nothing to do with the discovery of the body, and only knows what David and I have told her."

Caroline lifted her head and moved out of her mother's arms, but her gaze gleamed gratitude. The first of that emotion Laurel had seen from her daughter in a long time.

Hand on the doorknob the sheriff looked over his shoulder at the pair of them standing side by side. His dark eyes narrowed. Silence stretched long and thin.

"You sure about that?" he drawled at last.

Did he mean was she sure that she wanted to be present at any questioning of Caroline? Or was he implying that Caroline might know more about the situation than what she'd been told? The implications of the double-edged question slammed the brakes on Laurel's heartbeat and erased every thought in her head.

"You heard the lady."

The words from David rang as firm and defined as measured blows. Laurel's gaze widened. He wasn't a big man or taller than ordinary. The sheriff was twice his size, yet a quiet authority emanated from David that dwarfed the man behind the badge.

Did limitless money create that effect in a person? She didn't think so. Sure, money could buy a certain type of power. But David's was not that kind of presence. What sort of man—really—was this David Greene?

Sheriff O'Dell scowled and yanked the door open. "Let's get a move on, then."

"I'll throw on my jacket and boots and be right with you," David said.

The sheriff stomped out, trailed by gape-faced stares from his deputies. Apparently, they weren't used to seeing their boss bested in a contest of words and wills.

Laurel stifled a grin that would have mirrored the one Caroline wasn't hiding so well.

"I'll get those keys," Laurel said to David.

She darted for the bedroom and returned in short order. "Thank you," she said as she held out the vehicle's key chain. "I don't think I could face looking into that trunk again."

"You're welcome."

His fingers brushed hers as he accepted the keys. The warmth of the brief touch spread to Laurel's heart, and an odd expression passed over David's face. Like something scared him and pleased him at the same time. What was that all about?

David threw on his outerwear and hustled through the door, admitting another blast of cold air. The deputies closed in on her and Caroline.

Half an hour later, she swore she'd scream if anyone—anyone at all—asked her another question. Caroline was teary-eyed and using a tissue to swipe at her face while she huddled beside Laurel on the sofa. Neither she nor Caroline had any information to add to their insistence that, while they had known the woman in life, they had no idea how her dead body ended up in the trunk of their car. How many different ways could the same questions be asked, fishing for different answers? Each new angle of inquiry came like a fresh jab of the hook.

The sheriff stepped inside, red-faced from cold. He stood over them, steely eyed and radiating outdoor chill. "Who besides yourself, Ms. Adams, would have access to your car keys in order to get into your trunk?"

Laurel sucked in a breath. She hadn't been asked that one yet. "I carry a set in my purse and keep a set on top of my refrigerator at home."

"Do you keep your car locked at all times?"

"Always when I go somewhere. Almost always when it's at home in the garage. I suppose there is the rare occasion when I forget to lock it when I'm home."

Sheriff O'Dell rubbed his chin. Then his face

went blank. Was that a good or bad sign? Did her diligence to keep her car secured point more solidly toward Caroline and her as suspects?

"The ME has delivered his opinion that the victim was dead at the time the body was placed in the trunk. However, he was not able to estimate exact TOD due to—"

"TOD?"

"Time of death is as yet undetermined due to the frozen condition of the body. We should know more when the remains thaw."

Snuggled tight against her mother, Caroline's shiver at the grisly words transmitted to Laurel, but she resisted an echoing shudder and held her gaze steady against the sheriff's.

"Why are you telling us this?"

"Based on your collective statements, we are moving forward on the assumption that the body was placed into the trunk before you left Denver. Therefore, jurisdiction for this case will revert to the Denver P.D. However, if examination of the remains determines that the victim died after the time of your departure from Denver, jurisdiction may change. I have been in communication with the Denver P.D., and I'm afraid we'll have to impound the car for bumper-to-bumper forensic examination. I'm also going to have to ask both of you for every stitch of your clothing as well as your handbags and all of their contents."

"What?" Laurel heaved to her feet. "You can't leave us naked, without transportation and penniless!"

Sheriff O'Dell drew himself up stiffly. "I'm sorry. I have no choice. We must perform our due diligence to verify your story that neither of you had contact with the body."

"But our purses?"

"We must be thorough in sifting through possible forensic evidence. All of your belongings, including your car, will be delivered to the Denver Police Department. At some point, they will ask you for fingerprints and DNA samples."

Laurel deflated. "Caroline and I will put on the clothing we slept in. Don't worry. We borrowed those from our host." She glared toward the sheriff. "As your deputies have been told multiple times, we didn't move the suitcases after we found the body."

The man had the meager grace to drop his gaze. "One of my deputies can give you a ride back to your home in Denver."

Laurel opened her mouth, acceptance on her tongue, and then clamped her lips shut. Riding in the back of a squad car would turn them into a pair of caged canaries that the sheriff no doubt hoped might sing, or at least let slip a note or two that would offer up more information. The journey would be torture.

If only they had cell service out here, she could

call Janice to come get them. Of course, she could ask the police to use their radio, or even request use of David's CB radio, to send an officer to her friend's door with the request. That might be her only alternative, even though the delay might drive Caroline and her stir-crazy waiting in this cabin for Janice to arrive. They needed to get back to Denver—pronto!—and hire a lawyer.

Laurel opened her mouth to request assistance in contacting her friend, but a footfall brought her head around. David stood behind the sofa, groomed, shaved and attired in jeans and a Dallas Cowboys sweatshirt. A keychain dangled from one hand. Not hers; they must be his.

"I'll drive you and your daughter home right now."

Caroline sat up, eagerness painting her face, but the gently spoken offer rocked Laurel. Was she thrilled or appalled? Ride for hours in a vehicle with this too attractive and charming man who might be a murderer? Then again, David could be thinking the same thing about them. What better alternative did she have?

Silence throbbed in the enclosed space of David's SUV. They'd been on their way down the mountain for forty-five minutes and no one had said a word beyond the bare minimum.

The snowplow driver had been kind enough to open up a track from his garage to the driveway so they'd been able to head out in short order after the sheriff gave them permission. But not without that grim clichéd warning to Laurel and Caroline not to leave their home city once they arrived. The sheriff had even fixed his glare on David. "Best if you stay in the area, too, until the Denver P.D. gives you the word that you're no longer wanted for questioning."

So now he was a suspect again? Or at least "a person of interest." How could he not be when he was connected to the murder of another woman only a few short years ago? Sure, investigation would show that he'd had no contact with the Adamses or with Ms. Eldon prior to the previous night. But would that fact be enough to take him off the suspect list?

He'd see what his lawyer had to say about the situation. Did his passengers have a lawyer? Would they have a clue who to call when they got home? Why did he care when he had so much trouble of his own? But he did. Very much. He'd enjoyed coaxing smiles from them last evening, and he didn't wish on anyone the grinding legal and media persecution he'd faced, especially during those first months after Alicia was murdered. But despite his concern, he couldn't seem to bring himself to break the silence by asking if they needed help.

They were making reasonable time, considering the ferocity of the storm they'd just weathered. The highway had been plowed, but the pavement was sufficiently rough that David kept his speed well below the limit and his focus on the road.

Out of the corner of his eye, he stole a glance toward the occupant of the passenger seat. Laurel sat with her head back and eyes closed in a semblance of sleep, but the clamped-tight mouth betrayed awareness. He peeked in the rearview mirror and found Caroline snuggled against the door, head nestled on the pillow he'd urged her to bring along. A slack jaw indicated genuine sleep. He could be thankful for that much.

Laurel's thoughts had to be racing. Probably chasing the tail of one what-if after another. At least she had that aborted speaking engagement off her mind. As soon as they'd driven into an area with cell service she'd called the venue to let them know she couldn't make it. The person on the other end had told her that the storm continued to rage higher in the mountains with no sign of letup, and the event had been cancelled anyway.

"Thank the Lord for small mercies," she'd muttered and subsided against the headrest and closed her eyes.

Was she wondering what he'd really been up to last night? Or had she forgotten about the suspicious incident in light of more urgent matters with the police? If so, he'd be the one to thank the Lord for small mercies. If only he could reassure her that he hadn't done anything but look. Well, and snap a few photos of the tattoo with his phone camera. But far be it from him to be the one to bring the matter up.

"Where did you learn to play the piano so beautifully?"

Laurel had given up pretending to sleep and regarded him with solemn eyes. David drew a full breath into his lungs and smiled. This was a topic he could comfortably discuss.

"My mom. She was training to be a concert pianist until an accident badly damaged one finger and ended her chance at a career. Still, she retained enough skill to be a piano teacher, and she passed her love of music on to me."

"You were a lucky boy, then. I hope having her dream snatched away didn't sour her on life."

David chuckled. "Let's just say that the accident made her a very practical person. Not negative, but one to stare adversity in the face and make the best of circumstances with grace and dignity. If she'd gone on to join the New York Philharmonic Orchestra, which was her dream goal, I might not exist. She met and married my father when she returned to her hometown to rethink her life after leaving The Juilliard School."

"Juilliard?" Caroline chimed in from the backseat. "Way cool! It must have broken her heart to give up that opportunity."

David frowned. How hard *had* the experience been for his mom? It must have been tough, but she'd never spoken with grief about those days.

Maybe she'd been over the loss by the time he came along. Or maybe his boyhood shenanigans kept her too busy to dwell on the past.

"I'm not sure about that. I mean, it was probably a big blow at the time, but I kept her pretty busy. Let's just say that I was high spirited and leave it go at that."

Caroline giggled.

Laurel looked back at her daughter. "I had no idea you knew anything about The Juilliard School."

A beat of silence answered, followed by a miniscule sigh. "When we were little kids, Emily and I used to fantasize about becoming ballerinas."

"I remember." A smile grazed Laurel's lips.

"As we got old enough to go online, we looked up schools for dance, but by then we were just joking. We'd decided we'd sing our way to fame. Juilliard was like top billing for music, dance and drama, but it was a little uptight for a pair of budding pop stars. Besides, it costs like a bazillion dollars to go there. Your mom's folks must've been loaded, Mr. Greene."

"Caroline!" Laurel's tone was stern. "My apologies for my outspoken daughter."

"It's okay." David kept his tone gentle. How could he respond without wounding Caroline or offending her mother by dismissing her concern about good manners? "Mom actually came from dirt-poor stock—wrong side of the tracks even. All they owned was a little patch of farmland that no one thought was worth much at the time. She was at Juilliard on a full-ride scholarship. Maybe you think that makes the outcome all the more tragic, but I've always felt that what the world lost in a concert pianist I gained in the best mother a boy has ever had."

"Wo-o-ow!" The word exhaled from the teenager in slow syllables. "She must really be an awesome mom."

David's heart squeezed at the small sound from Laurel, as if she'd been struck. Caroline probably didn't even hear the low gasp.

"Yes, she was," he said, a lump growing in his throat. "Awesome, indeed."

"Was?" Laurel sent him a sidelong glance.

"She and my dad died in a car crash the day after I graduated from high school." His voice emerged rather thin as he forced the words past that persistent lump. "Dad was a good guy, too. He did the best he could with the handful I turned out to be and with running the mechanic shop that kept food on the table."

"I'm sorry to hear that your parents are gone." Laurel's words were as soft as a gauze bandage.

Warmth spread in David's chest. He glued his attention to the road that had become dry and clear as they reached lower elevations and left the storm zone. Here, snowy patches along the landscape were the exception rather than the rule, and his dash thermometer said the temps had risen to the mid-thirties.

"If they'd been around," he said, "maybe I wouldn't have gone so wild when I struck oil on the desert land my mom's half-Apache dad left me. The rights were private and the strike was big." David scowled and shook his head. "Grief and major money don't mix well."

Laurel pursed her lips then opened her mouth, but closed it and looked away.

David's heart sank. "That was probably way more than you wanted to know."

She smiled. "No, actually, it's very interesting. You speak of that lifestyle in the past tense. Something changed?"

David wrinkled his nose and let out a wry chuckle. "Let's just say my world caved in, and in the middle of the wreckage, a friend introduced me to his Best Friend. God changed me. No credit to myself."

"But you still don't know..." Her voice trailed away and a flush crept up her neck. She looked down and studied the fine-boned hands pressed against the sweatpants bagging around her slender frame.

"I've never made any secret that I have no memory of that last night with Alicia. You could well be riding down the highway with a guy who stole the life of another person."

Laurel's shoulders squared and her chin lifted. "For all you know, your passengers may have done the same thing."

"Oh, Mom, get real," Caroline burst out. "Mr. Greene knows we didn't kill Ms. Eldon."

"Does he?"

His face heated as her sober gaze fixed on him. What could he say? "I'm leaning toward faith in your innocence, but no, I don't know it for a fact."

"Fair enough." Laurel jerked a nod. "I want you to know that I believe that if you had a hand in your girlfriend's death there was no malice aforethought. I'd imagine the scenario was heat-of-the-moment, not premeditated, and not something you would be apt to do when in possession of your faculties."

"Thanks, I guess." He scratched the back of his neck. "That's more of a vote of confidence than most people give me. Now that we've acknowledged the elephant in the room, we can go back to ignoring it because it's not going away anytime soon. Tell me about the Single Parents Coalition."

Shadows receded from Laurel's eyes as she launched into an eloquent description of the nonprofit organization's mission and ministry. The conversation required little of him but the occasional nod or brief question. By her vivid description of the financial, social and emotional plight of many single parents—the majority of them women—and the resources her organization made available to these struggling people, David had no problem believing this woman was an engaging public speaker and a stellar fund-raiser for the cause. By the time they neared the outskirts of Denver, he was almost ready to dig out his wallet. Maybe someday he would make a substantial donation—if this current mess was ever straightened out favorably for all concerned.

A glance in the rearview mirror revealed that Caroline was catching a few more *z*'s. She'd probably heard her mother's spiel a thousand times. In sleep, the teenager's features relaxed into a picture of innocence and unformed promise. The girl could easily turn out as lovely as her mother. A smile tipped the edges of David's lips, then quickly faded. If someone was messing up her young life to cover up his or her crime, he wouldn't mind a few minutes alone with that person in a locked room.

Whoa! Where had that papa bear impulse come from?

Sure, he was prone to leap into a fray on behalf of the underdog—always had been. He'd brought home many a shiner from school to show for his impulsive protectiveness, as his parents could have attested. But he barely knew these people. Like he'd said, he didn't know for a fact that either of them was guiltless. He had to maintain his objectivity if he was going to investigate on his own.

"Where to?" he asked Laurel as cityscape began to slide past.

She provided timely directions for exits and turns, and they navigated to an upper-middle-class neighborhood of renovated historic homes in southeastern Denver. A police cruiser with bubbles whirling sat in the driveway of a rich tan-and-cream Victorian home on the corner of the block ahead. A breath hissed between his passenger's teeth.

"Your place?" he asked.

"I suppose they're executing a search warrant. They certainly worked fast."

He didn't bother to voice the thought, but in a murder case, the authorities seldom let grass grow under their feet. One thing, though, required a word of warning.

"Don't be surprised if they've left quite a mess in their wake. They're paid to take things apart and search high and low, not clean up after themselves."

Laurel groaned. "Just what I need. Welcome home!"

"I know how you feel."

They exchanged glances like a pair of old buds over a shared experience. The mutual sympathy set a warm glow around David's heart as he parked the Lexus LS and opened his door to winter's nip in the air outside. Laurel stepped out, pulling the jacket she'd borrowed from him close around her. Then she stared toward her home, a slump in those graceful shoulders.

Gut heavy, David opened the back door of the SUV to retrieve his jacket from the seat, and Caroline roused from sleep.

"We're here," he told her.

She sat up and looked around. "Oh, man, the cops made it already."

"Your mom and I noticed the same thing."

The girl's groan was a carbon copy of her mother's. "Here goes same song, second verse with new cops asking the same questions."

"Laurel! Caroline!"

The call came in a Deep South drawl. David looked up to find a tall brunette in low-heeled pumps, business slacks and a tailored, knee-length coat rushing up the sidewalk toward them.

"Janice!" Laurel hurried to the woman, who opened her arms, and they shared a hug.

"I'm so glad to see you home safe," the newcomer said, setting Laurel from her and looking her up and down.

Bundled in one of David's zippered sweatshirts, Caroline ran up to the women and collected an even bigger hug from Janice than her mother had received.

"You, too, hon," the woman said. "I heard about the storm in the mountains and worried my head off…then this." She flapped a hand toward the Adams home. "I'm so sorry."

Laurel's mouth drooped, and Caroline's gaze fell to the sidewalk.

"You know then," Laurel said.

"Know! I'm the one who called it in."

"What are you talking about?"

"What are *you* talking about? And why are you two dressed like Goodwill rejects?"

The woman took a step back with raised brows.

"That's my fault," David said as he joined them on the sidewalk. "I didn't have anything to lend them that fit better."

A pair of sharp green eyes assessed David, then her gaze transferred to Laurel. "You've never introduced me to this guy. A friend? Coworker? I didn't know anyone from the office accompanied you on the trip."

"No, he's not a friend. I—I mean we just met yesterday." Laurel's wide gaze flew from Janice to David and back again. "He's not with SPC. He's—"

"David Greene." He stepped forward, hand extended toward the brunette.

She took the hand in a firm grip. "Janice Swenson."

Her steady look betrayed no recognition. That was almost a first. She released his hand and looked past him toward the Lexus idling at the curb. Something indefinable sparked in the emerald gaze.

"There's got to be a whopping story behind this." She turned toward Laurel. "But first, you need to get on home and tell the police what's missing."

"Missing?" Laurel's face went blank.

"From your house. I stopped over about an hour ago to check that everything was locked up tight and…" Janice wrung manicured fingers together.

David suppressed a groan. This couldn't be good.

"Tell me." Laurel stiffened, chin high.

The posture was impossibly courageous despite

the baggy getup, and David's breath caught. He was a sucker for bravery.

"Someone broke in, honey." Lips quivering, Janice touched her friend's shoulder. "They jimmied open your deck door and made such a mess inside it's hard to tell if anything was taken or just all smashed up."

Caroline burst into tears and buried her face in her palms. David's hands fisted. Laurel wrapped her arms around her daughter, but stared over the child's shoulder into space as if she had no clue where she was anymore. Or even *who* she was.

Why did Caroline's meltdown and the devastation in Laurel's eyes make him want to deck someone? Maybe he hadn't changed as much as he'd hoped. Or maybe these two were getting under his skin.

David gritted his teeth. He couldn't let that happen. Caroline might be cute and feisty and fun and Laurel lovely, courageous and as graceful as his mother, but they were off-limits. They were on the suspect list in a case he was determined to investigate fully and fairly, and everything about them had to be examined objectively.

How he was going to pull off such mental and emotional gymnastics escaped him, especially since it was equally important that he stick as close to them as they would allow. Poking his head into the jaws of an alligator might be less risky, but how else could he keep his fingers on the pulse of this case while he dug for the truth?

FIVE

Laurel stood inside her front door and surveyed the wreckage of what had been a tidy foyer and tastefully appointed living room. Janice hadn't exaggerated the mess. Furniture was overturned—even the large pieces. Wall art was strewn across the floor, many of the frames broken, and the television looked as if someone had taken a baseball bat to it.

Why did Laurel feel nothing but tired? No outrage. No hurt. No sense of loss. Just…numb.

"Oh, Mo-o-m!"

Correction. Irritation was edging out numbness. Her daughter used those sing-song syllables for everything from excitement to teenage mockery. The drama was getting old, and the teen years had only begun. Then again, maybe her reaction was a surface symptom of emotional lava boiling beneath the surface.

Should she hang a sign around her neck to warn people? Danger! Blow imminent!

"It'll be okay, sugar." Janice put an arm around Caroline's shoulders, but her voice quivered. The devastation in Janice's eyes from absorbing the news of the murder had yet to fade, though the corners of her lips tilted staunchly upward.

"We'll get busy and set things right." She planted a kiss on the top of Caroline's head.

At least Laurel had her best friend to step in when her parental role began to fray around the edges. She'd tried to protect her daughter by directing her to go next door to Janice's house while she assessed the situation and dealt with the police. But no, the teenager had insisted on tagging along into the house.

"I'll help."

The quiet words in a masculine voice sent a shock through Laurel. They had another tagalong. Why was David Greene still here? Once he dropped them off, he'd been free to go. This was not his problem. She turned with words of thanks-but-no-thanks on her tongue but froze at the sight of a stranger coming through the door behind David.

She didn't recognize the newcomer, a tall rail of a man with graying hair and a salt-and-pepper mustache, but she didn't need to see the badge he flipped open to know that he was a cop. The seen-it-all-and-nothing-shocks-me calm in the slate blue of his eyes betrayed his profession. Plain clothes detective. Not the uniformed types that were leaving the house as she climbed the front stairs onto her porch. That pair hadn't said anything beyond a nod

Jill Elizabeth Nelson

and a terse Ma'am as they returned to their cruiser. Maybe this guy would be more communicative.

"Detective Roland Berg," he said. "You would be Laurel Adams?" His gaze fixed on her, and she nodded. "And this would be your daughter, Caroline—" he nodded toward the teenager "—and this must be Greene." Cold contempt ricocheted off David's frozen stare.

If an ice collision could generate sparks, Laurel wouldn't be surprised to see a few flying.

The detective returned his gaze to Laurel. "We heard you folks were on your way."

"Have you discovered any leads?" she asked. "Who might have done this? Why?"

Berg lowered his head and scratched behind his ear. "Seems we have quite a situation here. Mind if I ask you a question?"

"How about you answer her questions first." David's words were phrased as a suggestion, but rang with the same uncanny authority he'd used on Sheriff O'Dell in the mountain cabin.

The detective's shoulders lifted, as if deflecting an unexpected impact, and his lips turned downward, but he didn't shift his focus toward David. His gaze remained on Laurel.

"I'm a homicide detective, ma'am. I don't investigate burglaries, unless the two are connected."

"Don't you think they might be?" Laurel said. "Isn't it odd that two crimes involving us would occur so close on the heels of one another?"

"Odd is a good word choice. That was going to be my question. I'm sure you realize this *break-in*—" the two words were sharp edged "—taints any evidence regarding the murder that we might have found while executing this search warrant." He held up a piece of paper.

"I don't understand." The statement emerged on a pale thread of breath. Was the detective implying that she'd staged the vandalism to cover up murder?

"You sure about that, ma'am?" The detective's gaze ravaged her.

Laurel clamped her jaw closed. That's exactly what the man was hinting.

Did the detective think she'd walked around her home destroying her property before she drove off with a dead body in her trunk? And that Caroline helped her?

"Who is *we?*" David asked. "I only see *you* now that the uniforms called out on the burglary have left."

Berg smiled thinly. "My partner is having a walk around the yard, seeing what he can see. In the meantime, I thought I'd drop in and ask a few questions. Ms. Adams, do you always go away for a week and leave your security system unarmed?"

"What?" Laurel shook her head, not as a negative response but in denial of the question.

"When the uniformed officers arrived," he continued, "they discovered the security system was green light, as if someone was home. There was no evidence that the system had been tampered with. When the techs arrive we'll dust the buttons for fingerprints, but—"

Laurel spread her hands in front of her. "I never leave without arming the system. I distinctly remember setting it last thing before we pulled out of the garage."

The detective's blank stare delivered no assurance that her words were believed. Did this guy think she'd left the house unprotected from intruders on purpose? From his perspective, the suspicion made awful sense. What if the police never considered other options than her guilt—or her daughter's? A blow to the solar plexus couldn't have robbed her of oxygen more completely.

"Oh, sugar, I'm so sorry!" Janice pressed fingers to her lips, wide gaze on Laurel. "It may have been me who forgot to rearm the system. I came in here shortly after you left in order to grab the milk you told me to use up while you were gone."

Berg transferred his granite stare to Janice. "You have a key to this house and know the code for the security system?"

Did Laurel detect a hint of annoyance in the question? His pet theory was being shot in the foot. If this weren't poor timing for it, she'd wrap her friend in a bear hug.

"I surely do," Janice said. "Laurel and I have complete access to each other's places. We look after one another."

"Yeah." Caroline lifted her chin and linked her arm with Janice's. "And she takes care of me a lot when Mom's away on speaking engagements."

"Yet you went with your mother on this occasion? Why?"

Laurel shot her daughter a sharp look, and the girl had the grace to lower her head and remain silent. With the level of suspicion they were under, no one needed to start talking about bad grades and sour attitudes and troubled student/teacher relations.

"Detective Berg," Laurel said, "is it a crime to spend Thanksgiving with your daughter? Bringing her along was the only way that was going to happen." The statement was completely true, and she felt no compunction in making it.

The detective lifted a brow toward Janice. "Everything was in order in the house when you came inside following the Adams's departure?"

"Neat as the proverbial pin. My best friend keeps a beautiful home. She would never treat her things like this—" she waved a hand around the trashed living room "—any more than she would take another person's life. You should be out trying to catch whoever did both of these things." Janice's expression folded. "Provided the crimes are connected, of course."

"Let's assume so for the moment." Berg leveled his stare on Laurel. "Do you have any enemies, Ms. Adams?"

"N-no!"

Why that question should continue to take her by surprise, she didn't know. The deputies in the mountains had asked her the same thing, but she couldn't wrap her head around the possibility that someone might kill the teacher for the sole reason of framing her and/or Caroline for the murder.

"No," she proclaimed again. "I wish I could point you to the culprit, but I have no idea."

"People love my mom," Caroline said. "She helps them."

"Yes. The nonprofit organization. Single Parents Coalition?" The corners of the detective's lips tilted upward.

Sneer or smile? Laurel wasn't sure. "That's correct." Berg had done his homework prior to showing up here.

"You direct women and children to shelters, help them gain assistance to relocate and frequently provide legal aide. Could this be the work of a vindictive ex perhaps?"

Laurel's mouth went dry as a shiver rippled up her spine. *Steven!* Then she mentally grabbed herself by the nape. Yes, her ex-husband would easily have been capable of both the murder and the vandalism—of hiring it done anyway. He would have taken pleasure in masterminding anything to make her suffer, regardless of how his actions affected other people. But he couldn't be responsible for this. He'd been dead for years.

She squared her shoulders. "Yes, I suppose it's

possible that my work with the Coalition might have made someone angry, but I don't know of anyone in particular."

"We'll be interviewing your coworkers."

The weight in her chest lifted marginally. At least the authorities were going to check out other possibilities. Then her heart twisted. What if the media caught wind that one of the founders of SPC was involved in a murder case—was a suspect even? The organization didn't need any negative publicity affecting donations. Finances were tight as it was.

"How soon do you think the news services will pick up this story?" she asked the detective.

He cocked a grizzled eyebrow. "We're keeping the lid on it for the time being. At least until the victim's family can be notified."

"Where is Ms. Eldon's family? Where is she from?" David's questions fired sharp and staccato.

Laurel's gaze switched to his expectant face. Why was he so eager to hear about the teacher's roots?

"We don't—" the detective began and then halted as the front door opened, and a second man, younger but with that same cop look, stepped inside. "Anything?" Berg asked the newcomer.

The other detective rolled thick shoulders, full-moon face betraying no emotion. "Part of a hedge broken along the sidewalk between the garage and the house. Like someone ran through it. We could get the techs to check for fibers or other trace evidence."

"The hedge break happened two nights before we

left town," Laurel said. She exchanged a look with her daughter, whose cheeks reddened, though the girl said nothing.

"I was returning from an evening speaking engagement," Laurel continued, "when someone charged out of the dark and bowled me over into the bushes. I couldn't see his face, but he was wiry and not much taller than me, and his breath smelled like nacho chips. He got up and ran off without a word."

"Did you report the incident?" Berg's expression betrayed a spark of interest at her nod.

"A pair of uniformed officers came out the next morning and took pictures and looked around. I think they were the same two who were just here. You'll find a police report on file at the precinct."

Good thing Laurel had omitted from that report her suspicion that the nacho-snacking teenager fleeing the scene on her arrival home had been her daughter's guest. That matter needed to stay between Caroline and herself until she got a straight answer from the girl. She'd intended to bring the incident up as part of a long string of issues they needed to discuss while they were on retreat in the mountains.

"We have to ask you to leave the premises while our techs comb the property," said the second detective. "The van's en route." The last statement was spoken toward his partner, who nodded.

"Can't we at least go upstairs to our rooms and

change out of these clothes?" Laurel gestured toward her baggy sweatpants.

"We can't have you disturbing anything." The man's fierce scowl contrasted unpleasantly with Berg's frigid calm. "If you've got no place to go, we can get you a ride down to the station to wait. We'll probably want to talk to you some more anyway." A slight grin appeared.

Whatever happened to the good cop part of the routine? Apparently, she and Caroline had drawn bad cop/bad cop. Where was David with his quiet authority? Not that he'd be able to alter the rules of investigation, but he had a way of setting bully tactics in their place. Laurel looked around, but he'd disappeared. Did he sneak out the back door? She'd wanted him to go, but not that way.

"Never mind, hon," Janice said. "You all can hang out at my place and raid my closets. My clothes won't fit you much better than these, but at least you won't look like you belong in a homeless shelter."

Her familiar grin and wink injected a tang of normalcy into a tragic situation, and Laurel responded with a smile. "Throw in some lunch, and you've got a deal."

"My famous chicken and dumplings coming up."

Laurel patted her tummy. Hunger pangs had begun to gnaw. Or was the ache due more to anxiety? Either way, a little comfort food was in order for both herself and Caroline. Herding her daughter in front of her, Laurel headed for the door on Janice's heels.

"Don't go far," Berg said as they passed him.

Laurel turned on her heel. "If next door is too far, then arrest us and be done with it. If not, then don't bother us with any more of your insinuations." The big blow boiled on the edge of her self-control. Any more pressure might send her sky high. An explosion wasn't a wise way to handle the authorities, but she was nearly beyond caring. "Anything you want to know comes to us through our lawyer from now on."

She grabbed her daughter's hand and stepped onto the porch, where Janice waited. Laurel's skin pebbled as chilly air invaded the empty space between her legs and the fabric of her sweatpants. She pulled the door closed and exhaled long and hard.

Janice buffed her hands together. "Good for you, girlfriend, and good riddance. The nerve of those guys." She marched down the steps.

Caroline wrapped her arms around one of Laurel's. "Who's our lawyer, Mom?"

Peering into the anxious face just beginning to form into womanhood, Laurel's anger melted into anxiety. Who was their lawyer? She wished she knew. SPC had several attorneys on retainer, but none of them handled this type of criminal law.

"Don't worry, sweetheart. Let your mama figure that out."

Caroline released her and stepped back, face

scrunching into a scowl. "That's the sort of thing you always say, and I'm tired of being treated like a toddler. You quit being my *mama* by the time I was five years old."

The teenager stomped down the stairs and scurried after Janice, leaving Laurel stranded on the porch, mouth agape. Disrespectful didn't begin to describe her daughter's attitude. And yet, didn't Caroline also feel disrespected by Laurel's instinct to shield her?

Laurel's shoulders slumped. Why couldn't Caroline understand how much her mother wanted to spare her problems she didn't need to carry? What was so terrible about that? Didn't the girl realize how hard her mother was trying—and how close she was to falling apart? If someone had offered to carry this burden for her, Laurel would have been incredibly tempted to accept. But there was no one to fix this for her, or even share the load. As usual, she was on her own.

David stepped around the side of the porch, pocketing his cell phone. He hadn't meant to eavesdrop on the skirmish between mother and daughter, but they hadn't exactly kept their voices down, especially Caroline.

The girl was awfully hard on her mother, but as a perennial free spirit, he sympathized with Caroline's resentment toward her perception of being smothered. Of course, a little smothering kind of went with the mothering thing, and this was a crisis situation. Then again, Laurel's passion to protect her daughter and herself did occasionally drift into the territory of excessive. What had happened in the woman's life to anchor her in defensive mode?

Laurel was dawdling down the steps, gaze focused ahead but attention a million miles away. Clearing his throat, David stepped nearer.

She gasped. "Where have you been?"

If she hadn't meant the question as an accusation, she'd missed the mark. But coming up on a woman who'd been raked over the coals by the police and then taken a hit in an ongoing war with her teenager wasn't the best moment to find her in a mellow mood.

"As soon as the detectives started telling you to get lost, I stepped out back to call my lawyer in San Antonio."

"Good for you that you've got representation." She remained on the bottom step, her gaze now on a level with his.

David extended his lawyer's business card toward her, showing where he'd written on the back. "This is the Denver firm my lawyer suggests for you and Caroline. They're top flight. My cell number is below theirs in case you have any questions about walking through a murder case as the chief suspect." He offered a rueful half grin.

Her jaw slackened as she accepted the card. "Thank you. That was very thoughtful."

Surprise leaked through her tone. Wasn't she used to anyone doing nice things for her? Or maybe it was just him that she assumed incapable of a good deed. Evidently, sheltering them from the storm, lending them clothes and giving them a ride home hadn't managed to perch a white hat on his head. His lips flattened into a thin line.

"No, really!" She laid a hand on his shoulder, face softening, and a spurt of warmth went through him. "I'm...amazed...and appreciative. I'm sorry if I seem sharp edged. I must be growing a little shell-shocked at this constant barrage of terrible events." Her gaze dropped to the card. "I suppose these top-flight legal beagles are also top-drawer expensive."

"Lawyers are always expensive, but it can't hurt to give them a call and talk to them about your situation and their fees."

"No, I suppose it can't." Laurel offered a weak smile as she stepped down onto the sidewalk.

He looked away from her toward the pale pink Victorian house next door where Caroline and Janice had disappeared. While Laurel's home sported modest touches of gingerbread, one turreted tower and tooled spindles on the railing that skirted the wraparound porch, Janice's home took ornate to a new level—multiple towers and gables, plus gobs of gingerbread trim painted pastel blue in every available niche.

Laurel laughed, a pleasant sound that tingled up David's spine. He looked down at her.

"I read the expression on your face," she said. "Mine is more of an Edwardian style and hers is classic Queen Anne."

"You know a bit about architecture?"

"No, but Janice does, and she rarely withholds from me any scrap of information she possesses." The wry words were accompanied by a fond grin. "She's a real-estate agent and excellent at her job."

"I'll walk you over there."

"You don't ha—" She bit her lip and then nodded as they went up the sidewalk. "Thanks, but then you don't need to stick around. You've been more than kind already."

"Could you use a little extra muscle to help clean things up in there?" David gestured toward the house behind them. "When the cops say it's okay to go in, that is."

Laurel shook her head. "I may hire a company to clean up the mess. Insurance will probably pay. I wonder if the upstairs looks as bad." Her face paled. "Our rooms are up there, Caroline's and mine. I feel sick to my stomach thinking about anyone pawing through my personal things."

"I'd be surprised if you didn't react that way."

"And now the police are going to do the same."

She wrinkled her nose, which was a very cute expression on her. David mentally kicked himself for noticing.

"Mr. Greene, a word with you!" The bark from Detective Berg on the porch coincided with a van bearing the Denver police insignia pulling into the driveway.

David turned on his heel. "I think not. I gave my statement to the sheriff at my cabin, and I have nothing to add to it. You can refer any further questions to my lawyer."

He strode back to the porch and handed the detective one of his attorney's cards. Good thing he kept several on him at all times. A muscle jumped in Berg's jaw, but he said nothing as he snatched the card from David's hand.

Suppressing a grim smile, David swiveled away to find Laurel had gone on without him. A glance in the direction of Janice's house caught a glimpse of her disappearing inside. He had no good excuse to follow her. Why did that realization come with a pang?

Get a grip, buddy!

He climbed into his Lexus and drove away in search of the nearest decent hotel. David had packed a bag before the leaving the cabin, and had no intention of leaving town until he'd unearthed some kind of link between the dead school teacher and his murdered girlfriend.

If one existed.

How cruel would that be to have this hope of exoneration, then have it snatched away by some mundane explanation for the matching tattoos? No, he couldn't let himself think like that. There *had* to be a connection between the two women, but how was he going to dig it up? He knew only one person who fit the description of master sleuth who might actually be willing to believe him, but tracking Chris Mason down sometimes required skills on the level of the FBI or CIA.

An hour later, ensconced in a midrate hotel room where no one would expect to encounter a rich, notorious personage, he sat at the desk and took out his cell phone. A swipe and a tap brought up his photo gallery. He pulled up one of the photos he'd taken of the dead woman in Laurel Adams's trunk.

Swallowing bitter bile, he forced himself to study a torso shot of the murdered teacher. He could find no bruises on the throat to indicate that the woman was strangled as Alicia had been. No commonality there. In fact, other than the expression of pain or terror—or maybe both—frozen on the woman's face, there was no outward clue as to how she had died. When he'd leaned in to take the photo, he'd caught the barest whiff of an odd, burnt-almond scent. Poison? Only forensic examination might tell for sure.

He moved to the next photo and peered at the close-up of the tattoo beneath Ms. Eldon's collarbone. Snapping photos with a phone camera in the dead of night in the middle of a blizzard with only a flashlight for illumination didn't capture the best images, but this rendering was clear enough to make out the design of a bird's razor-sharp claws closed around a jewel.

In Melissa Eldon's case, the jewel was a ruby. Alicia's had been a sapphire, but there all difference ended. The claws were identical down to the striated ebony of the bird foot and the golden gleam of the talons. Logic leaped to the assumption that the same tattoo artist rendered both drawings. Didn't that bode well for a possible connection between the women?

David left his photo gallery and brought up his contacts. He had one phone number for Chris, who stood among the few friends he still possessed. Ironically, the friendship had formed as a direct result of the murder investigation that effectively murdered David's good name. More ironic still, David and Chris had gone to grade school together, though they weren't friends then. Who would guess David would come to like and respect one of the top investigative reporters in the world during a time when he regarded reporters on a level with the aphids that sometimes attacked his garden?

Actually, he owed Chris his life. If the man hadn't bluntly gotten into his face with the gospel David might easily have decided to end his personal pain in the final solution of death at his own hand.

However, none of that meant Chris would answer the phone when he called. Chris's job sometimes dictated undercover antics, and then he became incommunicado. Maybe his marriage a little over a year ago had changed the type of assignments he accepted. David could only hope.

Gut clenched, he hit the call button and listened to it ring. Once. Twice. Three times. At least he didn't get a message telling him the number was no longer in service. He should have stayed in better touch with his friend after the wedding instead of becoming absorbed in his own pursuits, but hermit habits can be hard to break, particularly when his natural inclinations were reinforced by outward circumstances.

"Mason here. This better rank right up there with a national emergency, David."

David expelled a spurt of laughter. No warm fuzzies with Chris, but the fact that the man answered when this wasn't a good time for a chat spoke volumes about their friendship. The knowledge might have put David in a cheerful mood except for the reason for his call.

"I'm in the loop in the murder of another woman, Chris."

A hissed-in breath, punctuated by traffic sounds in the background, said he'd grabbed his friend's attention.

"You a suspect?"

"Not this time—not yet, at least—but the body practically landed on my doorstep in the middle of a blizzard. In fact, the main suspects *did* land on my doorstep—with the victim in their car trunk."

Chris let out a low whistle. "Give me the thumbnail version."

"Why don't I cut to the chase? The woman in the

trunk had the same tattoo as Alicia did—and in the same spot under her collarbone."

"You think somebody may be offing women with similar tats?"

"Not just 'similar.' It's the *same* tattoo in every detail except the color of the jewel that the talons are holding."

"You think the two women may be connected." The words were a statement, not a question.

"I'm *hoping* they may be connected, and that the connection is related to the reason that they're dead. Because I *know* I didn't kill the schoolteacher in Laurel and Caroline's trunk."

"Laurel and Caroline?"

"The mother and daughter who rode out a blizzard with me in my cabin in the Rockies."

"You think they might have killed Alicia, too?"

"No!" David sucked in a breath. "I mean, I don't know. If they killed Melissa Eldon, one of Caroline's middle-school teachers, then maybe."

"But you don't think they did it."

"I'd prefer that not be the case. Besides, I can't think of any possible connection they could have with Alicia."

"Hmm." The sound was ripe with speculation. "I take it that Laurel isn't middle-aged and married."

"It's not that way."

"Okay."

Chris agreed too fast, and David ground his teeth together. "I just want some advice on how to uncover a connection between the two dead women that goes deeper than their tattoos. If that connection turns out to include Laurel, then so be it."

"Take it easy, buddy." Chris chuckled. "I'll—"

"Chri-i-i-is! Hurry!" A feminine wail sliced neatly through the conversation.

"Hang tough, honey. We're almost there."

Chris's assuring words had to be for his wife, Maddie, but David had never heard the ex-army communications officer in panic mode. Something really bad had to be going on.

"Sounds like I'd better let you go. Could you—"

"We're on our way to the hospital," Chris cut in. "My daughter is eager to be born. Let me—"

"Son!" Maddie's growl nipped David's ear.

"We went the old-fashioned way and chose not to know what we were getting," Chris said. "I need to turn off the outside world right now, including my Bluetooth, but I'll get back to you when I can."

"Don't call me. I'll call you?"

"Bingo, buddy! In the meantime, think location, location, location."

"What?"

"Look into this teacher's background, and compare it to what you know of Alicia's. If they were ever in the same place at the same time, that spot would be a good place to dig."

"But how do I find out Melissa Eldon's back—"

"Chri-i-i-is!"

The phone went silent.

David heaved a sigh, and then said a prayer for safe delivery of this gift from God into the world. Would he ever have the opportunity to hold a child of his own?

Before Alicia's death, parenthood was the furthest thing from his desire. A kid would cramp his lifestyle. After the crisis had humbled him enough to invite the Lord into his heart, he'd seen the world differently, and a new life to nurture took on growing appeal.

Except for one insurmountable obstacle.

Even if he knew for sure he hadn't killed Alicia—which he didn't—he'd never ask a woman to marry a murder suspect and live under that shadow with him, much less subject an innocent child to his stigma. Could this new development change his whole future, or was he destined to live out his days as a man without a family?

SIX

From the corner of her eye, Laurel studied her daughter. Caroline slouched in an easy chair in Janice's family room as far distant from her mother as possible. Beyond the curtains at the bay window, darkness gathered—an accurate reflection of the mood indoors.

Following an early supper, Janice had retired to her office, and Laurel and Caroline had listened to the radio news. Janice didn't care for televisions and didn't have one. Thankfully, there was no mention of the murder of Melissa Eldon or where her body was found. However, that circumstance would surely change sooner rather than later. Laurel had no clue how she would deal with the media.

At least they now had legal representation. She'd called the law firm David had recommended, and they'd assigned an attorney to the case. The first lawyer-client meeting wasn't until Monday, unless the police hassled them for more information between now and then.

A few minutes ago Janice had gone out for an evening house showing, leaving her guests to pretend absorption in their reading material of choice—a magazine for Caroline and a book for Laurel. So much ached to be said, but Laurel couldn't settle on an approach that would avoid the land mines strewn across the miles that stretched between her heart and her daughter's.

"Why can't we stay at our house?" Caroline suddenly spoke. "The police are done. They said we could go home. They even want us to take inventory and turn in a list of missing stuff."

"We'll do the inventory tomorrow, honey, after a good night's sleep some place where the deck door isn't broken so that anyone can walk in."

"Seems like they already did their worst. Why would they come back?"

"If I could answer that, I might know why someone vandalized our house in the first place." Laurel refrained from reminding her daughter about the possible connection between the vandal and whoever put the body in their trunk. "I thought you like to stay overnight at Janice's."

"I do, but tonight I wanted to sleep in my own bed. C'mon!"

"No can do, sweetie."

Caroline pouted her lips but the light in her eyes was more resigned than militant.

"I don't blame you for wanting a familiar bed," Laurel went on. "I do, too. But at least we were able to go in and get our clothes." She waved a hand over the comfy but well-fitting jeans and T-shirt she now wore.

She gave silent thanks that whoever trashed the downstairs had left the upstairs alone. Only the police had rifled through the personal belongings, and that was bad enough.

A grin flickered on the teenager's face. "Yeah. Mr. Greene is a neat guy and all, and Janice is cool, but wearing their clothes got a little weird. Could I just run home quick and get the pillows off my bed?"

The sweet plea in Caroline's eyes softened Laurel's resistance. "No, *you* can't, but *we* can. While we're at it, I might grab mine, too."

The girl jumped up, smacking her hands together. "All ri-i-ight!"

They threw on their jackets and went out into the chilly dusk. Caroline skipped ahead, bright head bobbing, all little girl for a sliver of time. Laurel smiled as she strode along, content to take up the rear. The streetlight on the corner lent plenty of illumination for the climb onto their front porch.

Laurel unlocked the door. Why she'd bothered to lock it after they collected their clothes this afternoon was a mystery, but the normal activity had made her feel better, so she'd gone with the impulse. She'd even armed the security system, even though the cardboard and Styrofoam over the broken pane of the deck door wouldn't keep a toddler out, and the security system would take no notice of the intrusion.

"If there's anything else you want, grab it now," she told her daughter as they trooped inside. "We're not making another trip tonight."

"Gotcha."

Laurel flipped the light switch for the pitch-dark foyer, but nothing happened. "Oh, bother!"

She'd forgotten that their burglar cum vandal had apparently taken the same baseball bat he'd used on the television to the light fixtures on the ceilings. There were no bulbs anymore on the ground floor. At least not whole ones.

"No worries, Mom." Caroline's voice coincided with her feet pounding up the stairs. "I'll get the light up here."

"Be careful!"

Laurel's call was overshadowed by the ring of the house phone. She frowned. The cordless set in the living room sounded muffled, as if it was buried under upended furniture. A light switched on at the top of the stairs and spilled a glow into the foyer, but there wasn't enough illumination for her to try picking her way through debris to grab the kitchen extension.

"I'm on it," Caroline chirped, and her footfalls faded down the hall toward her mother's bedroom.

Laurel hurried up the stairs. Her daughter was talking to someone as Laurel stepped into the master bedroom. Airy chintz curtains in pale blue print, warm maple furnishings and her down comforter swathing the bed conspired to welcome her home. Would it really be so foolish to spend the night in their beds? Caroline might have a point. Why would the burglar come back when he'd already done his worst?

"She's right here." Caroline carried the cordless handset toward her mother.

"Who is it?" Laurel mouthed.

Caroline rippled her shoulders in a shrug. With the heel of her palm over the receiver, she leaned toward Laurel. "Must be somebody you know," she whispered. "He knew my name. Real friendly, but I think he's got a bad cold."

Laurel took the handset. Had someone from the office already caught wind of their troubles? She intended to call Howard Brown, the director of the foundation, tomorrow and get his advice on how best to handle the situation to protect SPC. It would be just like Howard to get the jump on the issue and call her at home after hours.

"Hello?" she said.

"Hi, there," a masculine voice rasped. "Glad I caught you home."

It could be Howard with a bad cold, like Caroline said, but it was hard to tell.

"I'm going to grab my pillows," Caroline announced.

Laurel nodded, but her daughter was already out the door.

"Who is this?" she said into the receiver.

A scratchy chuckle answered. "We have a mutual acquaintance. Had one anyway. She went on to her just reward."

Laurel's throat seized. Was this Melissa Eldon's killer? What did he want with them?

"Surprised?" the man went on. "You shouldn't be. I see what you're up to with that lowlife Greene. Maybe you think he can protect you. He can't. He needs protection *from* you."

This guy was watching them? Where was he? In the house? Her pulse surged. Where was Caroline? On rubbery limbs, she staggered into the hall. Caroline's adolescent voice singing a current pop tune carried to her ears, along with the thud of opening and closing drawers.

Laurel stopped, gaze fixed on the stairs that loomed empty, ears tuned for a foreign sound anywhere in the house. Nothing but Caroline's singing.

"Who are you? Where are you?" She spoke the words in a fierce whisper.

"Look out your west window."

Bile burning her throat, Laurel backpedaled into the master bedroom and parted the chintz curtains. No dark figure lurked in the shadows below. A few yards away, the downstairs of Janice's house glowed with comforting light. How foolish could she be? Why had she allowed them to leave that haven of locked windows and doors?

Abruptly the light in Janice's family room winked

out. Laurel jerked as if struck. Her mind blanked, and then thoughts spun. A killer was in her friend's house, and it was her fault. She hadn't armed the security system or locked the door after them. What should she do? Would he come here next?

"Get out of Janice's house," she said, breathless as if she'd run a mile. "Leave us alone!"

Silence answered. The phone connection had been broken. Was this cold-blooded murderer on his way over? Would their dead bodies be discovered among the debris in the morning?

"Caroline!" The word rang with hysteria.

Now wasn't the time to worry about shielding her daughter from unnecessary alarm. It was time to let fear help them do whatever was necessary to protect themselves and call for help.

The ring tone sounded on David's cell phone, and he trotted out of the bathroom, toweling his wet hair. Chris was getting back to him faster than David had anticipated. Hopefully, that meant the birth had gone well. Which of the pair got their wish of gender? He smiled, congratulations on the tip of his tongue.

He picked up his phone, and the smile faded. Not Chris. The number on the screen wasn't one he recognized.

"Hello?"

"David?" It was Laurel, but her voice squeaked as if her windpipe was pinched. "Are you all right?"

"I'm fine. Why do you ask?"

"I just had a—" an audible swallow interrupted her words "—a threatening phone call."

The hairs at the nape of David's neck stood to attention. "Who was it? Where are you?"

"I don't know who it was. He talked like he had a bad head cold. Maybe he was just disguising his voice. Caroline and I are barricaded in my bedroom at our house."

"You're not at Janice's?"

"We came over to get some of our things, and then he called, and he was *there!*"

"At your house?" Every muscle went stiff. "Are you in danger?"

"No—well, maybe we're in danger. I don't know. What I meant to say was that he was at Janice's house. He told me to look out the window, and then he shut off the light in her family room—right where we'd been until we went next door. It's been a good ten minutes since then. Among the longest minutes of my life." She released a bone-weary sigh. "But I think if he was coming after us, he'd be here by now."

A muffled whimper sounded near at hand. "Tell Mr. Greene he needs to come right away."

Caroline wanted him there. His heart soared. If only someone would invent a teleportation device for moments like this. So help him, whoever was terrorizing this kid and her mother was going to answer for it. A growl formed in the back of David's throat, but he bottled it.

"Tell her I'll be there right away." He headed for the door, then froze and gazed down at himself. Every molecule screamed haste, but going out clad in nothing but a towel was certain to result in a detour to the nearest lockup.

"Don't worry about backtracking to our house," Laurel said. "The police are on the way. I called you because this…this *creature* mentioned your name."

"He knows me?" Frost touched his heart. Was Laurel and Caroline's connection to him putting them in greater danger?

"Everybody knows you, David. The point is, he's been watching us—Caroline and me—and he saw us with you. I figured if he'd left Janice's house and wasn't coming after *us*, he might be going after *you*. The card you gave me was in my pocket, so I called."

"No sign of any crazed killers—not that I've noticed, at any rate. I don't know how he'd find me anyway."

"You didn't go back to the cabin?"

"I'm at a hotel about five miles away. You can expect me on your doorstep as soon as I can get there. We need to talk face-to-face."

"Okay." The word sounded a little dazed and distant, as if she was listening to thoughts that were louder than his voice.

"The police are here." The thin squeal came from Caroline, and the connection went dead.

A long breath exhaled between David's teeth. No goodbye, but the woman had a lot going on. He dressed with the speed of a fireman on a callout and left the hotel room.

What kind of person thought about someone else's safety when she and her dearest family member could be in mortal danger? A selfless one, that's what. A genuine, caring human being—too unfortunately rare in this world.

David pushed the speed limit on the drive to Laurel's neighborhood. Déjà vu smote him as he pulled up to find a police car parked in her driveway. He got out and strode up the walk. Laurel's front door stood open, the back of a uniformed officer blocking most of the entryway. The officer held a lighted flashlight that lent some illumination to the porch. Voices carried to him, but not the sense of what they were saying.

A high-pitched cry greeted him as he reached the steps, and a slight figure rocketed past the officer and straight into him. Reflexively he hugged the quivering teenager.

"Hang in there, kiddo." He patted her on the back. "We're going to figure this out."

She gazed up at him. Traces of wetness on her cheeks reflected the glimmer of the bubble light wheeling atop the squad car behind them. David's heart twisted.

She sniffed and rubbed at her face. "Maybe you can give Mom a hand with the cops. They went into Janice's house, guns drawn, all cop-show style, but didn't find anybody. One of them is trying to figure out why the light won't come on in the family room, while this guy—" she jerked her head in the officer's direction "—talks to Mom. With all the same questions asked twenty times different ways, she's about to tear her hair out. What happened to yours?"

"My what?"

"Your hair."

David put a hand on the top of his head and found a damp rat's nest. He'd known there was something he forgot in his rush out the door. "Just showered and haven't run a comb through it."

The officer at the door turned, tucking an electronic notebook into his pocket. "We'll file the report, ma'am."

Laurel came out after him, arms hugging her jacket-clad body. "Will you at least do more frequent drive-bys tonight?"

"That'll be up to the captain, ma'am. I'll put in the request."

The officer swiveled his head forward as he headed across the porch, then pulled himself to a halt nearly chest to chest with David. The policeman was stockier and about half a foot taller but he took a step back. David's jaw clenched. He seemed to have that effect on people.

"You done over here, Josh?" The voice came from behind them.

David turned to find a second officer standing on the sidewalk.

"Took a statement," said the first cop. "What did you find over there?"

"Blown fuse. These old houses, you know." He shrugged and smiled toward Laurel.

"But the phone call," she said. "He told me to look out the window, and the light went out just like that."

Officer number two shook his head. "There's no evidence anyone was there."

"But you do believe me about the call."

Josh pulled his electronic notebook from his pocket and tapped it a few times. "Just verifying my memory. Your caller ID shows a call coming in at that time from an unregistered number. Probably one of those throwaway cell phones."

"So you won't be able to get a lead on his identity from it?"

"Sorry, ma'am." Josh frowned.

At least he looked genuinely apologetic about that.

David cleared his throat. "Don't worry about keeping an eye on the ladies tonight. I'll make sure they're safe."

"How do you plan to go about that, sir?" Officer Josh's nostrils flared.

"Yeah," said Caroline, but she sounded intrigued rather than skeptical.

David looked toward Laurel, who was staring at him with her eyes narrowed and lips parted. "I plan to work out those details with Ms. Adams, thank you."

Josh grunted and trooped down the porch steps. The other officer followed, shaking his head.

David turned his back on them. "Would you and Caroline prefer to move into a suite at the Hotel Monaco, where the security is excellent, or would you rather I call a security company and have them send their best man to camp out in a van at the curb while you get some decent shut-eye?"

"David, I can't afford either option." Laurel planted her hands on her hips.

"I can."

"This is not your problem."

"Isn't it? I'm up to my neck in this murder and mayhem, especially now that this joker is dropping my name into your ear. Keeping you and your daughter safe is my top priority while the authorities track down whoever is terrorizing you and sees me as part of the equation."

"Thank you very much, Mr. Greene, for the vote of confidence in our department's investigative abilities." Detective Berg's voice carried to them out of the dark, and then his form took shape, striding toward them across Laurel's winter-crisp lawn. "Even if you seem less sure about our success in providing protection," he added.

Laurel gasped, and Caroline grabbed her mother's arm.

"I'm operating on an assumption," David said, "or perhaps it's more like a desperate hope, that the Denver P.D. will do a better job of solving this case than the San Antonio P.D. did with mine."

"Then you'll be happy to know that there's been progress." Berg planted one foot on the bottom step and crossed his arms.

"What?" Laurel stepped forward. Under the moonlight, her breath puffed little white spurts into the cool air.

"I heard on the police band radio the report of this alleged incident and thought I'd drop over with an update."

"Alleged?" Laurel's tone went shrill.

Berg spread his hands. "Everything is alleged until it's been verified and documented, Ms. Adams."

David would give a three dollar bill for the genuineness of the smile beneath the detective's shark stare.

"Let's have the news you came to give us," he said.

"Ms. Adams, do I have your permission to speak in front of this unauthorized person?"

"You do." Laurel edged closer to David. He repressed a grin…and the urge to grab her hand in his.

"In that case," said Berg, "I'll share with all of you that the forensics team has determined the lock was broken on the deck door of your home from the inside."

"What?"

"Huh?"

Laurel's and Caroline's exclamations erupted simultaneously. The breath left David's lungs as if he'd been sucker punched.

The detective planted both feet on the ground. "Whoever broke the lock was already inside the house when they did it." His gaze sifted through each of them. "Whenever you want to come clean with what's really going on, you know where I am. But rest assured, we'll find out, with or without your cooperation. Have a nice night."

Berg turned on his heel and strode away.

Mouth agape, David's gaze followed his lanky figure into the darkness. Did this development mean he should believe the worst about Laurel and Caroline when he'd just begun to believe the best?

SEVEN

A sob spurted between Laurel's lips. She staggered to the porch railing and leaned into it, gripping with both hands.

"I can't believe this is happening. The blows keep coming. What is going on?"

"Oh, Mo-o-om!"

Caroline's arms wrapped around Laurel, and she turned to hold her shuddering daughter. At least this time the child sought the parent rather than the virtual stranger, David Greene. She knew it was petty to be jealous when she'd leaned on the very same man for comfort herself, but the question still rang through her head. Why had Caroline formed a bond with this man—equating him with safety, rather than her mother? Hadn't Laurel spent her life attempting to provide security and stability for her daughter?

She looked over at David. He stood head down, still as a post, with his hands in his jeans pockets. She may not be comfortable with the way Caroline had taken to the man, but she couldn't deny that having him around made her feel safer, too. That is, if he was planning to stay after what the detective had just revealed. What must he think of them now?

"I think," he began, then halted, lifting his head and meeting her gaze as if he'd heard her silent question. "I think someone very clever is doing his best to ensure suspicion sticks to you forever, whether or not you are convicted of a crime."

A degree of tension unwound in Laurel's middle. At least he continued to give them the benefit of the doubt.

If his words hinted at a potential correlation between his situation and theirs, she was willing to concede the point—to a degree. Not that the cases were related, but that it was possible for what seemed apparent—her and Caroline's guilt—not to be true at all. It was as if she and Caroline were now walking the proverbial mile in David's shoes. Should that put to rest in her mind any suspicion of his guilt?

If only the problem were that simple. She *knew* she and Caroline were innocent, but with the sort of man David Greene was before the Lord entered his life, how could she lay down caution entirely? Then again, when he did and said so many right things, how could she stop her heart from warming toward him?

"At the moment," she said, "the vote of confidence means more than we can say."

"Yeah, what she said." Caroline scrubbed the heels of her hands against her eyes.

Laurel touched her daughter's thin shoulder. "Let's get those pillows we came over for and then scoot back to Janice's house. Maybe David would be kind enough to walk us home."

"Happy to do it." He smiled. "I take it you've chosen the independent security service option."

"Nothing of the sort." She opened the door and motioned them to enter the foyer.

Caroline breezed through, but David waved Laurel to precede him. She complied, but then turned toward him and found herself within inches of his lean, athletic frame. The light filtering down from the upstairs hallway illuminated his face. Staring into those ocean-fog eyes, she attempted to speak but her tongue seemed trapped behind her teeth.

She hauled in a deep breath and took a step backward. Time to assert her independence. Becoming more beholden to David Greene than they already were was not an option.

"Since there was no intruder in Janice's house," she said, "Caroline and I should be perfectly safe there until our own home can be made secure again. Janice has a pretty sophisticated security system, and believe me, I plan to upgrade mine as a part of the necessary repairs."

He nodded. "Sounds like a wise plan. Would it be too intrusive of me to ask for your cell number in case I need to call you there?"

"I suppose not. I'll enter your number in mine while we're at it." Her hands dived into her jacket pockets, but didn't find the cell, only the card with David's number on it. "I guess I left my phone at Janice's. Here's my number anyway." She rattled off the digits, and he entered them into his contact list.

The tap of feet on the stairs brought her head around to find Caroline trotting down with pillows puffing around her as if she'd become part marshmallow.

"Here, Mom." As she reached the bottom of the steps, Caroline thrust one toward her.

"That's it then?" David asked.

"I think so." Laurel nodded.

She was careful to turn out all the lights and lock the door. Then they trooped next door. As they neared Janice's porch her car turned in to the driveway, and the door of the detached garage rattled upward.

"As you can see," Laurel told David, "our hostess is home. She's a graduate of our local police academy's self-defense class, so I think we'll be fine."

He chuckled—a warm sound that feathered an unexpected peace around Laurel's heart. "Then I guess I can head back to the hotel for some shuteye."

"Thanks for everything," Laurel said.

"Yeah, thanks, Mr. Greene." Caroline waved.

"You're more than welcome." David lifted a hand, then strode away.

For some odd reason, the night seemed colder without his presence. Suppressing a shiver, Laurel followed her daughter up the porch steps.

"Oh, say!"

Laurel turned at David's call. The outline of his figure showed at the end of the walk.

"I know you said you might hire the cleanup done at your place, but there will still be some things you'll want to handle in person. May I give you a hand in the morning with whatever needs doing?"

Laurel laughed. "You want permission to be put to work?"

"That's about the size of it." A grin carried in his tone.

"Yes," she said, and then bit her lip as a second thought whispered no.

"Great!"

His enthusiasm dampened her impulse to retract her permission. What could it hurt to have a strong back around if they wanted to set some furniture to rights while cataloging missing property for the police and the insurance company?

"Come at ten. The insurance adjuster is supposed to show up at nine in order to photograph the damages. I don't want to touch anything until after that."

"You got it."

David left and Laurel went inside. Welcome warmth enfolded her until a chill grazed her heart at her daughter's excited chatter to Janice about their scare this evening. Laurel joined them in the kitchen.

Janice's stunned gaze traveled to Laurel. "This is seriously bent! What is going on?"

"My question exactly."

"I haven't gotten to the worst part," Caroline piped in.

"The worst part?" Janice blinked.

"We had another visit from Detective Berg," Laurel said. "He thought it necessary to drop by and tell us that whoever broke the glass and the lock on our deck door did it from the *inside,* not the outside."

Janice gasped.

"Way weird, huh?" said Caroline. "How are the cops going to catch whoever did it if they aren't looking because they think *we* did it?"

Janice shook her head slowly, as if recovering from a knock to the skull. "Let's check out the family room. This house may be old and overdue for an electrical upgrade, but I rarely have issues with blown fuses."

Without stripping off her coat, she led the way to the family room. Laurel followed on weighted feet. What if the uniformed officers had been too quick to dismiss the intrusion?

Janice stood in the middle of the room and did a slow-motion three-hundred-sixty-degree scan of the area. Laurel held her breath, and from the corner of her eye, caught Caroline gnawing her lower lip.

Their friend flapped her arms against her sides.

"I don't see anyth— No, wait!" She pointed toward the fireplace mantelpiece. "Did either of you change the order of the frames?"

Laurel's gaze traveled over the framed eight-by-tens and five-by-sevens of butterflies and moths collected and mounted by Janice's late husband along with photos of Janice at fun activities with friends. There were no family photos. The woman didn't have any close relatives left in this world, one of the common denominators of their relationship and a reason they so dearly treasured one another.

"I didn't," Caroline spoke up.

"Me either."

Janice walked over to the mantle. "I'm almost positive the locations of the framed butterflies at either end have been switched, but when you see something every day, you tend not to register the details. Could I have changed the arrangement when I dusted last? I don't remember, but as you can tell—" she swiped at the mantle's surface and displayed a mottled fingertip "—I haven't dusted recently."

Laurel stepped closer and studied the spots where the photos met the surface of the wood. "I don't see any disturbance in the dust like what might happen if someone moved the frames."

Janice blew out a breath. "Probably just a false alarm. Anyone on board for some popcorn and cocoa?"

"Me!" Caroline's hand shot up.

"Come on, sugar, and give me a hand in the kitchen."

The pair scuttled off, chattering and chuckling. The happy sounds grated on Laurel. Not that she begrudged a lighthearted moment to the people she loved most in the world, but the displaced photos bothered her.

The frames appeared to sit squarely in undisturbed dust. And yet, since these two frames were identical in size and style, it might be possible for a meticulous person to lift them and make the switch in such a manner that it would be impossible to tell the deed had been done unless someone remembered the exact order of the pictures before they were changed.

Laurel closed her eyes, conjuring up a mental image of the mantelpiece and the display. Her recollection proved sketchier than Janice's. She couldn't have said in what order any of the items were placed. An exasperated sound puffed from her chest.

Should she call David and take him up on his offer of professional security services? Sweat dampened her upper lip.

She patted her pockets, hunting for her cell phone, and discovered she was still wearing her winter jacket. No wonder she was sweating. She shrugged out of it on her way to the foyer closet. There sat her cell phone on the small table next to the closet door. Had she put it there? She couldn't remember, but she must have. Was she losing her mind or what?

Giving herself a mental scold, she hung up her jacket then reached for her phone. It gave a muted buzz and vibrated in her hand. She let out a little cry as her heart rammed her rib cage. The number in the caller ID screen wasn't in her contact list. Another call from their evil tormentor? Then recognition set in as the phone continued to buzz in her hand. David's number.

She swiped the screen to answer. "Hello?"

"I called to confess," he said without preamble.

"What?"

"In about ten minutes, if you look out Janice's front window, you'll see a van parked across the street. Don't be alarmed. It's supposed to be there. The guy inside won't budge all night."

"You called a security company?"

"I couldn't sleep otherwise. Forgive me?"

Laurel stood stock still. What should she say? *That's great that you ordered security surveillance without my permission. I was thinking about calling and asking for it anyway.* Maybe she would have decided to call a security service herself and pay for it out of her meager savings. Or maybe she would have decided against hiring private protection. Now she would never know what she would have decided.

"David, I think I'm angry right now. Give me space to think this over."

"Fair enough. Can I still come over tomorrow?"

"Yes… I mean no… Oh, for pity's sake, come ahead. If nothing else, we need to talk about what role, if any, you can have in this matter going forward."

"All right. I'll be there."

Laurel broke the connection. Carrying the phone, she stalked into the family room and flopped into an easy chair. The hum of a microwave and popping noises drifted from the kitchen.

Was she really angry or just bewildered and overwhelmed? The poor guy had sounded meek as a kitten when he'd apologized for doing a good deed.

Or maybe a too-good-to-be-true deed.

Did he have some personal agenda, or did he genuinely care? If the latter, *why* did he care? Didn't it make more sense for someone in his position to distance himself from someone in Caroline's and her situation?

Laurel's temples began to throb. She sank lower into the chair, laid her head back against the cushion and closed her eyes. Enough trying to figure out the world tonight.

Tomorrow, if the insurance guy gave the green light, she needed to get on the phone and hunt for a contractor who would come and repair their deck door. But with tomorrow being the day before Thanksgiving, she held little hope of seeing the task completed so she could be back in her own home for the holiday.

The phone in her hand gave a slight tone. She looked at the screen, but it wasn't a call. It was a text message. Who now? A sensation like fingers gripping her throat took hold of her, but she shook her head and sat up. She tapped to bring up the text. It was David giving her the phone number of Mack Simmons, the guy in the security van, in case they needed to call him in the night. Another tally mark for David in the thoughtful column.

A sigh flowed from her depths. She had to get a grip on her emotions. She couldn't live in fear of phone communication for the rest of her life. Besides, the creep who was terrorizing them had called on their landline. She had no reason to believe he had her cell-phone number.

Or did she? Her heart froze in her chest.

The phone had vibrated when David called. Vibrated! She might not remember exactly where she set her phone down, but she knew for a fact that the ringer had not been set on vibrate. As if scorched, Laurel flung the instrument from her. The phone thumped to the carpet, and the screen lit, mocking her with its glare.

She couldn't prove it to a soul, but Melissa Eldon's killer had handled her phone. He now knew how to call her wherever she was whenever he wanted.

David gave up on sleep by two in the morning. He couldn't get a leash on questions that chased each other around his brain. Sitting on the edge of the bed, he scrubbed his fingers through his hair and then switched on the bedside light.

Chris hadn't called yet, but he'd told David to

look into Melissa Eldon's background. David was no computer whiz, preferring his keyboard work to be on the piano, but he knew the basics of running a search engine. It couldn't hurt to check the internet regarding the tattooed teacher. At his mountain cabin he hadn't bothered to take his laptop out of his vehicle since there was no internet service, and now it sat neglected in the corner of his hotel room.

He unpacked it and fired it up, then logged in to the hotel's Wi-Fi system. His first stop was White Pages to see if he could find out where Melissa Eldon had lived. The address came up as an apartment complex. Unsurprising for a teacher new in town. The listing offered no associated family members, so she could well be a single woman living alone or with an unrelated roommate. Research into the place revealed it to be an upper-middle-class sort of rental located not far from his hotel. The lead warranted a stop tomorrow to see if any of Melissa's neighbors or the landlord could give him information about the woman's background.

He left White Pages and typed "Melissa Eldon" into the bar of a search engine. There was a Melissa Eldon on Facebook and LinkedIn, the former a more social listing, the latter primarily about business. He clicked through the links on each. *Bingo!* Both featured the smiling face of the deceased teacher, but precious little information was offered to someone without Friend or Connection status.

David studied the photo of Ms. Eldon when she'd

been alive. The woman had been stunning in a pale and aloof sort of way. No glasses, and the thick blond hair was pulled away from the diamond-shaped face in an updo caught by an ornate hair clip. The smile was movie star quality, but lacked warmth. Either she'd been born with the gift of perfect teeth, or her orthodontic work had been excellent.

Something about the eyes arrested him. Nothing physical like the color, which was the pristine blue of a mountain lake, but an aura he knew too well. He'd glimpsed the look in Alicia's eyes in rare moments when giddy fun faded and reality intruded. And he'd seen that look in his own eyes when he was sober and gazed into the mirror during those bitter years after his parents' deaths and before he found comfort and acceptance in his relationship with Jesus Christ. Haunted emptiness engraved the look…framed by desperation to fill that emptiness by any means necessary.

Such a mindset created a taker, not a giver. Melissa Eldon might not have been the nicest person. Could she have made someone angry enough to kill her? She sure rubbed Caroline the wrong way. Or was this not a crime of passion? The disposition of the body spoke of cold calculation in implicating someone else for the crime—provided he continued to give Laurel and Caroline the benefit of the doubt.

The police were skeptical about the "alleged" phone call to Laurel, and David supposed that could have been staged. The home-wrecking could also have been staged, just like the detectives thought. Then why did Laurel's and Caroline's reactions ring so true? And what possible connection could they have to Alicia? Until he had proof positive of their guilt, he was going to operate on an assumption of their innocence. It was the least he could do when he was all too familiar with the onus of the assumption of guilt.

A yawn overtook him, and he stretched with both arms. Maybe he could actually sleep now.

One more pit stop on the Net before he crawled between the sheets. He had neglected to ask Laurel or Caroline the name of the school where Melissa Eldon taught. However, local newspapers sometimes featured articles on teachers new to town. The name of her school would be in that article, supplying him with one more avenue to research. Maybe Denver was too cosmopolitan for the newspapers to run such down-home articles, but the local paper in his rural Texas hometown had done it every year. It didn't hurt to check.

He brought up the website of the *Denver Post* and clicked on Archives, then entered "Melissa Eldon." An item appeared dated earlier this month. It wasn't a feature article on teachers. Not hardly. And it wasn't so much the brief text of the piece that socked him like a punch between the eyes. It was the bold, living color photo.

Ms. Eldon had been very busy since her arrival

in Denver, not in class preparation, but the dating game. She'd recently become engaged to be married—to a man that David knew.

A bit beefy and a little balding, the man standing next to Melissa Eldon in the engagement photo stood shoulders back and head high, though the top of his head barely reached his lady love's nose. The last time David saw this man—the only time they'd met, actually—the guy wasn't happy. He was blubbering into his champagne cocktail. Literally. David's memory of the incident played a haunting chorus on his emotions—embarrassment, discomfortand sympathy.

Melissa Eldon had apparently made a happy man of Gilbert Montel, the richest man in Colorado. David could about imagine what losing her to a murderer might have done to this melancholy millionaire. As much as he hated to intrude on grief—or subject himself to a repeat of their original encounter nearly four years ago—Gil Montel was exactly the person he needed to see. If anyone in Denver was likely to know details of Ms. Eldon's background, it would be her bereaved fiancé.

EIGHT

Laurel awoke with a headache throbbing behind her eyes. Little wonder when she hadn't slept well for several days. But this was not a day she could afford to sleep in. She glanced at the clock on the bedside table. At least she'd slept past her normal rising time of six. It was nearing eight o'clock. She forced her legs to swing out of bed and sat up.

Shower first, and then coffee. Lots of it—hot, black and strong. The insurance adjuster would be at her house in one hour. She showered and dressed, then went for that coffee. By the coffeemaker sat a note from Janice. She'd gone for an appointment, but thought she'd be back before lunchtime.

There was no sign of Caroline. At least one of them was catching up on z's. Last night before turning in, Laurel had made her daughter aware of the appointment with the insurance adjuster today, so when Caroline finally shook off her beauty sleep, she'd know where to find her mother.

Sipping at her brew and nibbling on a slice of

toast, Laurel sat at her friend's bedroom vanity and applied her makeup, then used a blow drier and a round brush on her shoulder-length bob. Good thing the thick mane didn't require much effort to be presentable.

At five minutes to nine, she threw on her jacket and stepped out of Janice's house into the sunshine of another brisk day. Stepping off the porch, she stopped and eyed a black van parked across the street. The rear door opened and a linebacker-size man hopped onto the pavement, pulling a stocking cap over his ears.

He sauntered across the street, small grin on his beefy face. "Mack Simmons, ma'am. All quiet last night."

He held out his hand, and she shook it. The scarred knuckles suggesting a brawling background—probably a good thing in a bodyguard.

"Laurel Adams. Thank you for keeping watch. Were you warm enough out here all night?"

"Toasty. There's a heater in the back where I hang out. Refrigerator, port-a-biff, all the comforts of home." His grin broadened, and she couldn't help but warm to this character. "I'll be back tonight. Have a good day."

He trotted to the van, started the vehicle and drove off.

This was a good arrangement. During the day, she didn't have to feel watched, and at night...well, maybe she'd let herself sleep better tonight. She'd been crabby with David on the phone about the bodyguard thing. Maybe she should lighten up and be grateful—though she still intended to find a way to repay him for his expenses.

Laurel crossed the frozen lawn and inhaled a deep breath as she unlocked the door. *Please God, no unpleasant surprises here today.* What she walked into was no surprise, but it still brought a groan to her lips. The frightful mess hadn't grown less shocking with the passage of a day.

A deep bong echoed in Laurel's ears, and she jumped half a foot. What a goose! It was only the doorbell. Swallowing her heart back into place, she opened the door. A portly man of medium height, dressed in a suit and holding a clipboard and a camera, stood on her porch. At the intensity of his frown, her heart sank.

"Associated Insurance Representative Leonard Stern here," he said, though the name sounded more like "Ledderd Sterd," as if his nose were stuffed up solid.

The effect sent the creepy-crawlies up Laurel's spine. The man who called to threaten them last night had sounded as if he had a cold. Though his voice had been lower and raspy, the coincidence was enough to put her on edge. Maybe she should have asked David to come over an hour earlier so he could be here for the inspection. Straightening her spine, she mentally scolded herself for absurdity.

"Hello, Mr. Stern." Laurel extended her palm.

The man shook it with a flabby hand and a flab-
bier grip. "I trust we can expedite this matter.
My family is supposed to be on the road to my
wife's parents' for Thanksgiving weekend. If we
get started after ten o'clock, we'll never make it by
dusk. I despise driving after dark."

"Come in."

Laurel stepped back, and he sailed past her.
Pleasant day to you, too! She kept the sarcasm to
herself. It didn't pay to antagonize the man in charge
of her claim, however much she might like to vent
on someone.

"My, my! Someone did a number on this place."
The man continued tut-tutting as he began picking
his way through the house making check marks
and notes on forms, as well as snapping pictures.

Laurel followed him from room to room…at a
safe distance. They reached the kitchen, and she
bit her lip, eyes and nose stinging as the odor of
spilled milk ripening on the floor reached her nostrils. Though the door to the refrigerator was closed,
the entirety of its contents had been flung around
the room. Eggs and jelly and other types of food
decorated the walls and floor.

"Your vandal certainly was thorough," said Stern.
"Anything missing, ma'am?"

Had a smidgeon of sympathy leaked into his attitude?

Laurel cleared her throat. "We haven't had a
chance to sort through anything yet. We couldn't

touch the mess until after the police had finished their investigation. That didn't happen until late yesterday afternoon, and we—my daughter and I— were too tired to face it."

Stern pursed his lips. "I understand. Perhaps you will have the opportunity today. Here's my card. You can fax, email or phone a list of damaged and missing items to my office. I won't be there, of course, until Monday, but by then we should have the police report and can finalize a benefit figure."

"Police report?" Pulse accelerating, Laurel studied the business card.

"Of course. We must have a reasonable determination from them that the damage occurred as a result of the actions of a third party, not the insured themselves." The man actually smiled in a semi-sympathetic way. "You'd be surprised how many fraudulent claims we get."

"No…um, I probably wouldn't be surprised."

Did she look as pale as she felt? Given Detective Berg's opinion of her and Caroline, as well as the forensic determination that the broken sliding door was an inside job, what were the chances of being cleared of suspicion by the authorities? Probably about the same as a snowball surviving July.

"I thought I'd hire people to come in and clean up the mess," she said. "Do I have to wait until after the insurance company makes its determination?"

"No, I've got what we need." He lifted his clipboard and camera. "But the work will have to be on your dime until we authorize a check."

"Of course." Laurel's heart fell. As if she'd ever see that check. She'd either have to say goodbye to more of her savings or else take on the cleanup task herself.

"Very good, then." She squared her shoulders.

"I'll let myself out," he said with a wave. "The turkey awaits." His round face creased in a grin at the prospect of getting on with his holiday plans.

With the adjuster's disappearance, Laurel slumped against the counter. What holiday plans did she have? Neither Janice nor she possessed any culinary skills, so it would probably be overdone turkey and lumpy mashed potatoes served with an unhealthy helping of dread.

What could she possibly do to protect her daughter, much less herself, from this juggernaut of events arranged by some malicious mastermind? *God help us!*

The tears that had stung her eyes at the sight of the kitchen spilled onto her cheeks, tracing twin rivulets to her chin. She didn't bother wiping her face as a sob shook her shoulders. Might as well lose it right here and right now, while she had a few precious minutes alone, before—

A footfall crunched glass somewhere behind her, and a scream squeaked between her lips. She whirled to find David standing in the kitchen doorway, hands raised.

"It's just me. I called out when I stepped inside, but I guess you didn't hear me."

His gentle words warmed her ears and her heart, but her head rebelled against such a siren song. She turned away, squashing sobs that swarmed in her throat.

"If anyone deserves a good cry, it's you, Laurel."

Unexpected understanding and acceptance broke her resolve, and she melted to the floor, where she hugged her legs tight to her chest and wept into her knees. A hand fell on her shoulder and stayed there as the storm swept through. At last the bitter sobs began to fade into soft hiccups. She lifted her head and scrubbed fiercely at wet cheeks. David was sitting next to her on the floor, head down, lips moving soundlessly.

When was the last time someone prayed for her? Sure, the staff prayed together regularly at the office during morning devotions, but those prayers were usually for the ministry and for those they served. Of course, she hoped that Janice and other friends included her in their prayers, but she didn't *know* it. Not like this. Not with someone plopped on the floor alongside her in the middle of her mess.

"Thanks." The word croaked between her lips, but it had been a while since the simple statement of gratitude had been so heartfelt toward another human being. Or toward God, if she were honest with herself. She needed to fix that.

"Don't worry about it," he said. "I'm not too great

at dealing with tears…not the way folks like you make a life out of comforting others."

A watery chuckle left her lips. "You did perfect."

Their gazes met and held. Laurel's mouth went dry, and her breath came in small spurts. When had this particular shade of gray—warm and smooth and enveloping—become her favorite color? Their faces drifted toward each other…closer…closer…

"Mo-o-om!"

Caroline's call rang through Laurel's head. She jerked back and gasped. David's head turned toward the doorway, and Laurel's gaze followed his. Caroline trooped into the kitchen dressed in jeans and a sweatshirt, hair in a ponytail.

"What are you doing on the floor?" She blinked at them.

"Um…oh…I don't—"

"We were inspecting the damage," David interrupted Laurel's stammer. "These eggs are dried onto the walls and floor. It'll take a lot of scrubbing to get them off."

Laurel grabbed the edge of the counter and pulled herself to her feet. David rose beside her.

"I'm afraid with dried eggs scrubbing won't be sufficient," she said. "We'll have to paint and may have to retile the floor."

"Oh, man, what a bother!" Caroline frowned. "What smells so bad?"

"Sour milk," Laurel answered, gesturing toward

the empty jug in the middle of curdled glops on the floor.

"Milk?" David drew his brows together. "I thought Janice told the police she took your milk home."

Laurel opened her mouth, but nothing came out. Janice *had* said that she'd come into the house to get the milk. Had she been lying to protect Caroline and her? It wasn't like her friend to stray from the truth, but perhaps in her mind, the cause had been sufficient.

"I'll ask her about it. In the meantime, we might as well do what we can to get this place livable again."

Caroline's shoulders slumped. "I thought you were going to hire some cleaners."

"I may have to rethink that." She shook her head as she decided to keep her answer vague. Explaining that they may not receive any insurance reimbursement would stress Caroline and might prompt an unwanted offer of financial assistance from David.

"Besides," she went on, "it might be good therapy for us to roll up our sleeves and put a little sweat equity into our own place. We have to catalog missing items anyway, so we might as well pick up as we go."

"I'm in." Caroline stood to attention.

"Me, too," David said. "The cleaning part anyway. And don't tell me I don't have to do this."

"Well, you don't." A smile formed on Laurel's

face. "But I'm not going to turn you down." David grinned, and Laurel's heart performed cartwheels. She looked away quickly. "The cleaning supplies are in the pantry, but who knows what mayhem we'll find in there."

So much for defining boundaries with him as she'd intended to do today. How could she resist his sympathetic willingness to help?

David opened the pantry door. "What do you know? The vandal missed this area."

Caroline clapped her hands, while Laurel thanked the Lord under her breath. In short order, she had handed out cleaning implements and supplies and assigned duties. She gave herself the chore of the kitchen and sent her daughter and David to the living room and dining room. Caroline could catalog any missing items while the male muscle set furniture to rights. Meanwhile, the tough scrubbing jobs would give Laurel time to think.

On her hands and knees with scrub bucket by her side, she attacked the smelly milk puddles and dried eggs on the floor. What was up with Janice's fabrication about coming in to get the milk and forgetting to reset the alarm system? Had she been here at all? If not, how did the security system get deactivated? There must be some other explanation than an outright lie.

Laurel would have been willing to swear that she'd armed the system when they left for her speaking engagement. Yet, the more she strained to recall every detail of their departure, the less she was sure of anything. Recent events blurred with dozens of other trips. But even if she *had* been the one to leave the security system unarmed, how would a prospective burglar become aware of her oversight, and how would they get into the house in the first place without damaging doors, locks or windows?

The spare set of keys on top of the refrigerator! Laurel hissed in a breath.

Of course, the burglar would have needed to be inside before he could access those. Or maybe, just maybe, he'd found a way to get them prior to the break-in. If that was the case, then their burglar and, theoretically, Melissa Eldon's killer, could be someone she knew—someone she'd invited into her home. A coworker? A friend? A friend of a friend? There'd been that Labor Day barbecue she'd hosted for the SPC staff and their families. Lots of people had been in and out of the house, and she didn't know everyone personally.

If the keys were missing, wouldn't that suggest to Detective Berg and his partner that someone else would have had access to the house and to the trunk of her car? She hadn't looked at those keys for close to a year and wouldn't have known they were gone. Lots of people had second sets lying around that they never bothered with unless there was an emergency.

She righted an upended kitchen chair. *Please,*

God, don't let those keys be there. She dragged the chair to the refrigerator and climbed onto it. Holding her breath, she peered over the top of the fridge.

The layer of dust was downright intimidating. Janice's mantelpiece had nothing on the top of Laurel's refrigerator. There was no way anyone could move a set of keys and later replace them without creating telltale marks in the dust.

Laurel let out a long groan. There they sat, mocking her. This ring of keys held access to both the house and the car, and it hadn't been moved. The only other person who had a key to the house was Janice, and even she didn't have keys to Laurel's car. Besides, she was the friend who had apparently lied to protect Caroline and her. No! She wasn't going to start suspecting Janice of dishonesty. There had to be some other explanation. Janice was more than a friend. She was the sister Laurel never had. Janice had proved more than faithful over the years and deserved Laurel's trust.

Besides, there was a worse implication for the presence of the keys, undisturbed, where she always kept them. Only the set of keys attached to the car remote control that was kept securely in her purse could have been used to access both the house and the trunk of her car.

The finger of suspicion pointed squarely back at her or Caroline—or both of them—and Laurel saw no way to prove their innocence.

* * *

"Of all the rotten tricks!" Caroline stood, pale and sober, surveying the keyboard of the small piano in the dining room. "Something sticky has been poured all over the keys."

Stomach roiling, David looked over her shoulder. In his book, sabotaging a musical instrument was lower than low, but venting his anger in front of Caroline wouldn't help her deal with her feelings. Neither would downplaying the damage.

"You're right," he said in even tones. "There's a sick mind at work here." He brushed a finger across a key, then smelled the residue on his finger. "Honey, I think. It'll be a nasty job to clean up, particularly between the keys. You'll need to hire a professional. I'll give my office assistant a call and have her track someone down who won't charge you an arm and a leg."

"Thanks, Mr. Greene." A smile touched her face, then faded. "I keep wondering how we're going to get through this. Everything looks so bad."

David patted her shoulder. "I don't pretend to know how, but I do know Who. In some form or fashion we may not be able to fathom right now, God will bring good out of what someone meant for evil."

The small smile reappeared. "I've also heard that sometimes we have our part to do in order to make that happen."

"Then let's get busy."

Together, they attacked the mess, armed with a dustpan for scooping up broken glass, multiple garbage bags and old-fashioned muscle and effort. Some of the wall art was salvageable, but none of the frames. The television was a goner, too, but the DVD player had been spared. Knickknacks were mostly in pieces.

"I hope none of these were keepsakes," David said, holding up a decapitated china figurine.

Caroline frowned and let loose one of those expressive sighs teenagers the world over have perfected. Evidently, the figurines of women in elegant gowns—five of them—had been special.

"Those were Janice's. Mom admired them, so Janice gave them to Mom for a birthday present the first year she was our neighbor. Mom thought the world of her 'elegant ladies' as she called them."

Heart heavy, David added the figurines to the contents of a garbage bag. "So you and your mother moved to this neighborhood first?"

"We'd been here a couple of years when Janice and her husband bought the house next door. It had stood vacant for a while, but they fixed it up. Mom had to do the same for this place. It was kinda dumpy when we got it. Not run-down, but the decor was totally last century." The final words came with an eye roll.

David chuckled, then grunted as he righted a tipped easy chair. "Your mom must be handy with a paintbrush and savvy about home decorating."

"She can even wield a mean hammer—just don't trust her with a cook pot." Caroline laughed. "Since we're putting things in order, let's rearrange the furniture."

"Your wish is my command, milady." David winked and Caroline giggled. "Grab one end of the sofa. We'll set it upright and then you show me where you want it."

Of course, Laurel might pitch a fit and make them un-rearrange, but the extra work was worth it to make the teenager happy for a little while. Actually, he should be honored Laurel had assigned him to work with Caroline. Laurel must have decided he was at least somewhat trustworthy if she allowed him to be in the same room alone with her child.

Progress in one area called for progress in another, but his gut pinched together as he cast about in his mind for a way to fish for information. What kind of a louse stepped in to help so he could get closer to clues? He *did* care about Laurel and Caroline, but he also needed to uncover the truth, and he was a long way from ready to let anyone in on the common denominator between the two dead women.

They wrestled the sofa into its proper orientation. The cushions remained strewn on the floor, but that was an easy fix. He grabbed one and tossed it to Caroline for positioning.

"You're a good kid, smart, hardworking. Anybody can see that. But school can be a pain for other reasons. Do I get the vibe that's what's going on with you?"

Caroline scowled as she scooped up another cushion. "It's not schoolwork so much as people."

"People? Other kids? You're not being bullied, are you?"

"Nothing like that."

Her cheeks reddened as she turned and deposited the cushion on the couch. The haste of her answer and the fact that she avoided meeting his eyes suggested otherwise.

"If someone is picking on you at school, you should tell your mother."

The girl snorted and whirled toward him. "And have the parental tsunami unleashed on every unsuspecting student, teacher and administrator in the place? The survivors would never speak to me again!"

David bent and retrieved the last cushion—part of his strategy not to be caught smiling at the teenage drama. Not that bullying was a laughing matter. Quite the opposite. And it certainly wasn't something that Caroline should continue to deal with on her own. She needed to talk to the appropriate people, and the first appropriate person was Laurel, not him. But he could understand her fears that Laurel might go overboard. He could tell she was a very protective mother, and she wouldn't sit idly by if she thought her daughter was being harmed. She also might not stop to consider that drawing too much attention to herself was the last thing Caroline wanted or needed.

He straightened and handed Caroline the last cushion. She fit it into the empty space and plumped it into place with more violence than necessary.

"You don't trust your mother to be discrete?" he said softly.

She plopped onto the sofa and crossed her arms, lower lip drooping in the suspicion of a pout. "She'll mean to, but it won't turn out that way. She's a crusader and gets hyper when someone is being mistreated, especially if that someone is me."

David eased onto the sofa beside the girl. "So someone *is* bothering you."

"Not some*one*. Some*ones*. And it's not bullying. It's more like...pressure." She kept her gaze averted and her voice to a near whisper.

"Pressure to do what?"

"Go out with a guy I don't like."

"Your mother allows you to date?" David's eyebrows strained toward his hairline.

"Of course not." She whipped her head toward him, eyes wide. "But some of the girls meet boys they like at the mall and stuff. They say they're going to hang out with friends, and then they just don't tell their parents that they split off when they get there to hang with a guy."

"Your friends are pressuring you to do that...and with someone you don't like?"

"Not *my* friends. His!"

Comprehension settled over David, and he sat quietly for several heartbeats. "So this boy likes you and wants you to hang out with him at the mall, but you've told him you're not interested, so he's got his buds pestering you to give in."

Caroline didn't say anything, just stared at her toes and nodded.

"That's got to be hard to live with every day. Who is this jerk?"

"Just a guy you wouldn't know." The girl pressed her lips together.

David frowned. "You need to tell your mom. She's your best ally in a situation like this. I'll give you a day or two to spill and then I won't be able to keep it to myself any longer. Your mother should speak to this kid's parents before Thanksgiving weekend is over. And if that doesn't work, she needs to go to the school administration."

"You're kidding me, right? I'm more likely to get disciplined than he is."

"Why?"

"Because his dad practically funds our private school."

"You don't go to public school?"

"Mom thinks I'll have a safer environment at a faith-based school."

"Which one would that be?"

"Grace Academy, a couple miles from here. For once, I'm glad they don't do bus service. That way

I don't have to deal with harassment on the way to and from school."

"No buses? How do you get there?"

"The parents team together in rotating car pools. Personally, it seems like a pain for all concerned. Sometimes when it's my mom's turn she has a real hard time working it into her schedule. Sometimes she can't. If it weren't for Janice—"

"Did someone speak my name?" Laurel's neighbor, wrapped in her tweed coat, popped into the room on a waft of chilly air.

"Janice!" Caroline leaped from the couch and ran into the woman's open arms. "Did you sell a house today?"

"I think I might have, sugar." Janice kept an arm around the teenager's shoulder. "We'll hear from the bank about financing right after the holiday weekend. Now I'm free to be your mom's slave for the rest of the day."

Caroline giggled.

"Where is she, by the way?"

The question was spoken to Caroline, but Janice's gaze settled on David. A part interest, part loathing expression crossed her face.

"She's in the kitchen," he said before Caroline could answer. "Cleaning up spilled milk."

He emphasized the word milk and narrowed his gaze. If this woman already found him disgusting, he might as well draw her ire on the milk issue, rather than putting Laurel in the position of antagonizing her friend with suspicions. Unfortunately, he couldn't fool himself about having purely self-sacrificing motives. He wanted answers for personal reasons.

Comprehension flowed into Janice's eyes, and she smacked her forehead. "I can't believe I forgot."

She hustled toward the kitchen, and David followed, Caroline in his wake. Laurel was sitting on a chair next to the refrigerator, scrub brush in hand, bucket full of sudsy water by her feet, but it didn't appear she'd made much progress on cleaning the floor.

Arms in the air, Janice did a slow turn in the middle of the mess. "Ooooe, hon, I am so sorry. If I'd actually taken the milk, at least it wouldn't smell like a sour cream factory in here."

Laurel rose. "You didn't take the milk?"

"Well, duh!" She gestured toward the empty jug. "I mean, I *did* come in after it, but I got a phone call from a client before I even opened the fridge. Big sale potential. He yacked my ear off so long I wandered on out without grabbing the milk. I *thought* I rearmed the alarm system. It's so second nature, you know, but I must have been too distracted. Can you ever forgive me?"

Beaming, Laurel wrapped her friend in a hug. "With you, I can picture the whole thing happening. I did wonder for a few minutes if you'd lied in order to protect Caroline and me."

Janice chuckled. "You know I'd wrestle an alligator for you two, but I draw the line at lying to the cops."

"I'm glad about that." Laurel clapped her hands. "Of course, you're forgiven, but if you really want to do penance you can help me clean this up."

"You got it, sugar. Let me run home and change into my grubbies."

David and Caroline parted in the doorway as the woman hustled out between them.

"I knew it." Laurel met David's gaze. "A completely reasonable explanation, especially if you know her."

"That's great." David smiled.

And it was—for the sake of Laurel's friendship with someone she cared about. But Ms. Realtor wasn't off his suspect list yet. Maybe Laurel hadn't realized it yet, but if no other suspects emerged, she and Caroline remained squarely in the crosshairs of the investigation.

For that matter, he had no way to be sure that this trio of females wasn't in cahoots on disposing of Melissa Eldon. Motive was pretty hazy yet. Dislike of a teacher's personality wasn't sufficient for murder, unless there was more going on than they were willing to say. And how did any of this connect to Alicia? He had to keep digging, but the more he was around Laurel and Caroline the more he *wanted* to be around them. He'd hate to find out they weren't the innocent victims of a devious frame-up.

But if they weren't guilty, who was?

NINE

"Thank you for your help today," Laurel said as she walked David to the front door after a delivery-pizza lunch.

"Glad to do it. Sorry I have to run off like this. There are a few things I need to handle this afternoon."

He smiled, and her feet seemed to take leave of the floor. What was up with the teeny-bopper reaction? And why did his gaze dart away from hers so quickly? Was he nervous? That niggling sense that he knew something he wasn't telling her anchored her shoes to the tile.

"'Bye, Mr. Green." Caroline came up beside Laurel as David stepped outside.

"See you, squirt." David turned and winked, but it wasn't a playful wink. A searching stare accompanied it.

Caroline suddenly found fascination in the toes of her tennis shoes. More secrets? Laurel frowned as she watched David retreat up their sidewalk. What had her child and David talked about while they straightened the living room and dining room?

Laurel closed the door and turned, mouth open to ask, but Caroline had disappeared like a puff of smoke. Small sounds from the girl's bedroom betrayed her location, but Laurel restrained herself from pursuit. She'd give the teenager a little space and see if she came clean. If not, Laurel might have to kick up some dust with her daughter and with David.

She was alone in the downstairs now. Janice had left for her home office to deal with some work. Heaviness weighed Laurel like a lead mantle. Shoulders bowed, she retreated to the kitchen and began a third scrubbing of the kitchen floor. She might not have to replace the tile if she could get the last traces of egg to fade a bit more.

"Mo-o-om?"

Caroline's tentative, almost frightened tone brought Laurel's head up. Her daughter was standing in the doorway twisting her fingers together.

Laurel rested on her haunches. Wary didn't begin to describe her body and mind. "Did you find something missing or damaged upstairs?"

The teenager lowered her gaze and shook her head. Laurel dropped her scrub brush into the bucket and rose. She mopped at her forehead with a gloved hand and left a wet streak behind to mingle with the sweat she had meant to brush away. No matter. She stripped off her gloves and dropped them to the floor. Whatever this was with her daughter looked serious.

"Come sit down. I'm all ears."

She pulled out a pair of chairs from the kitchen table. Caroline sat, fingers twined on her lap, gaze averted. Laurel held her tongue and waited, harder to do than one would think when everything within her strained to know what was gnawing at her precious child.

"What would you do," the teenager began as if treading on verbal egg shells, "if someone who thinks they're all that was trying to get you to do something you didn't want to do?"

Laurel laid a hand over her daughter's. "Sweetheart, you know I believe in standing up to a bully, but I also believe that sometimes we need help to do it. Is someone giving you a hard time?"

"But what if they could maybe hurt more people than just you if you didn't do what they wanted?" Caroline peered up at her with knotted brows. "I know you also believe in protecting the innocent even if it costs you something. I've seen you sacrifice lots of times, especially when it comes to me."

Warmth spread in Laurel's chest and battled the chill in her stomach. Caroline had taken note of her mother's sacrifices whether she said thank you or not, but now that very ethic, passed on to her daughter, was conflicting with self-preservation. Her mommyness dictated that she go to war with whatever or whoever threatened her child, but Caroline seemed genuinely worried about the potential consequences. Diplomacy might do the job better.

"I need more information in order to answer your question, honey."

Caroline removed her fingers from beneath her mother's and used them to tuck stray strands of hair behind both ears. "Mr. Greene said I should trust you."

Laurel's backbone went stick straight. "You talked to David about this?"

"Only a little," Caroline said hastily. "He's pretty good at asking questions and figuring stuff out, even when a person doesn't say much. Kind of like you, which is why I haven't said *anything*. But he told me if I didn't talk to you, he was going to do it."

Laurel sat back, air gushing from her lungs. She should want to hug David for fostering a breakthrough, but honestly, right now she'd rather slap him. How irrational was that? He'd given her daughter the proper advice—talk to your mother. But Laurel was pea-green jealous—and hurt—that Caroline had opened up to *him* first.

Laurel swallowed a sour lump from her throat. "Tell me what?"

Caroline shook her head. "I don't want to name names. I just want some advice about a situation. Haven't you often told me you want me to grow up confident and able to stand on my own two feet?"

"I can respect that, but you need to remember

you're thirteen and still need a parent to help with some things."

Her daughter nodded. "How about this? You give me advice, and I'll try it out. If it doesn't work, then I'll tell you more. Deal?" Caroline extended her hand.

How could Laurel stay grumpy in the presence of such earnest maturity? She smiled and clasped her daughter's hand. "Deal. Now, what's the situation?"

Laurel's eyes widened as Caroline outlined a scenario of a teenage crush that had gone overboard. Of course, she couldn't blame a young man for becoming infatuated with her lovely daughter, but daily persecution wasn't acceptable. The boy must be spoiled rotten and stuck on himself. Unfortunately, Grace Academy was full of kids who fit that description. The enrollment list was a close reflection of the country club roster—the only saving grace was that the quality of education was of the caliber to match.

"How do I get this lame jerk off my case?" Caroline spread her hands. "Telling him no doesn't seem to make a dent in his ego. He thinks I'm playing hard to get."

Laurel pursed her lips, then cocked her head. "How about this? Take Janice to school with you on Monday and let her give him the royal smackdown."

She smirked, and the haunted look faded from Caroline's eyes as she let out a giggle.

"That would be way fun!"

Good, her joke had worked to lighten the mood—but now she needed to be sure Caroline understood what was at stake. "Sure, while it lasted, but Janice might land in a pile of trouble."

"I guess we won't go with that idea." Another giggle escaped, then faded. "For real now, what should I do?"

Laurel gazed into her daughter's expectant face, and her heart swelled. *David, I owe you big-time.* Caroline hadn't looked at her with such trust and openness in months. No doubt, mother and daughter still had tensions and growing pains to work out between them, but Laurel savored the moment.

"Tell him yes."

"Huh?" Caroline's eyes widened.

"But here are the stipulations to your agreement. Number one, your mother or your mother's best friend will accompany you on any outing."

"Mo-o-om, he'll think I'm a dweeb!"

"What do you care what he thinks as long as he lets you alone?"

"I guess." She sounded half-convinced.

"Number two," Laurel went on, "his parents are also to be invited, whether they come or not will be up to them."

Caroline brightened. "I like that, but he's only got one—" She clapped a hand over her mouth.

"Giving away clues as to his identity, are we?" Laurel smiled. "Never mind. These days, a great many kids have only one parent in the picture. Let's stick to business. Number three—and this is the zinger—the only time you two can be together without a parent or Janice is at your youth group meetings at church every week. And if he wants your friendship, he must attend those."

Caroline's mouth dropped open, then she jumped up with a squeal and threw her arms around Laurel's neck. "Brilliant!" She danced around the room, clapping. "My mother the genius! He'll hate that one worst of all."

Laurel's heart sang even as it sank. Caroline hadn't given her such a spontaneous hug in a long time, and she was desperately proud of her daughter for resisting peer pressure. But that sorry young man had so many strikes against him. Either a mom or a dad was absent from his life, he clearly had too much privilege without being taught about responsibility and, despite attending a faith-based school, it seemed he had no spiritual roots to anchor him for the storms of life.

Laurel rose. "Someday you'll tell me this character's identity?"

"Someday."

They grinned at each other and smacked a high five.

The house phone rang, and still smiling, Laurel went to the kitchen extension on a corner of the counter. Caller ID showed the SPC office. Someone among the holiday skeleton crew must have caught wind that she was at home and hadn't reached the site for her speaking engagement. The weather report for the Rocky Mountains would be enough to explain that without any inkling about the trouble in which she and Caroline had landed.

At least, Laurel hoped that was the case. She wanted to break the news about their involvement in Ms. Eldon's case herself, and had been putting off the conversation with Howard, the organization's no-nonsense administrator. Had she waited too long?

She picked up the handset. "This is Laurel."

"Don't come in to the office until the media attention dies down," Howard said without preamble. "You should be able to work from home well enough."

"Media attention?" Laurel's stomach plummeted to the floor.

"You didn't watch the noon news?"

"I've been a little busy and haven't had access to a television. While Caroline and I were away, someone broke in to our house and trashed the place."

Howard sucked in an audible breath. "I'm sorry to hear it, Laurel. The police didn't say anything about that. They were here this morning asking questions. Didn't give us much information except to say that a dead body was discovered in the trunk of your car. The noon news supplied the woman's identity, and the newshounds are on the scent of a sensational story—camping out on SPC's doorstep already. I'm surprised they haven't been to your house yet."

The doorbell pealed loud and long.

"Mo-o-om!" Caroline's cry carried from the living room. "There's a news truck outside, and some guy with shaggy hair and a camera on his shoulder is walking around our lawn."

"I think they're here," Laurel said to Howard as tremors swept through her bones.

On the drive over to Gilbert Montel's estate on the outskirts of the city, David mulled over his morning spent cleaning up the results of savagery. He'd overheard Laurel calling contractors, hoping to find someone willing to come that day to fix the sliding door to the patio and change the locks throughout the house. So far, the project was a no-go until after the holiday weekend. Even the security company couldn't schedule a system upgrade until next week sometime.

David wasn't surprised. It looked as if Laurel and Caroline would make Janice's house their home for the next few days.

At noon, relaxing into easy camaraderie over steaming slices of delivered pizza, he'd realized he was enjoying himself too much for his peace of mind. Why did he have to like Laurel and Caroline so much when he couldn't allow himself to fully trust them? Even Janice seemed to have put her reservations about him on hold and was downright funny with a wacky sense of humor that cheered

Laurel and Caroline no end. He'd found himself feeling grateful to the woman.

Not that he could trust *her* either. Naturally, Laurel would buy any explanation approaching reasonable that her friend supplied, but to his way of thinking, her response to the milk issue was both too vague and too pat. Then again, the subjective nature of Janice's explanation could be the best argument that it was genuine.

Pain shot through his jaw, and he commanded himself to cease grinding his teeth. *God, I need to find answers pretty soon, or I may have no teeth left!*

As David pulled up at the gate of Gil's acreage enclosed behind high walls, he forced from his mind the troubling issue of his relationship, if one could call it that, with the Adams females. He rolled down his window and pressed the button on the communication box. A full minute passed, then finally a brisk female voice laced with a vague brogue inquired who he was and what he wanted. Housekeeper, most likely.

"David Greene," he answered. "I'm an acquaintance of Gil's. I'd like to offer my condolences in person."

A beat of silence followed. "That's most kind of you, I'm sure," the woman said. "But Mr. Montel and young Grant have gone out of town for the Thanksgiving holiday."

Grant? Oh, yes, that was Gil's son. The man had

mentioned his boy a couple of times during their emotion-laden encounter in the hotel bar after a day of sessions at an investor's symposium in Dallas.

"I'm sorry to have missed them." Disappointment tasted foul on his tongue. "I'll come back another time."

"You do that. They will be home on Friday."

At least he didn't have to wait until Monday to make contact with Gil. Just another lonely Thanksgiving Day to endure between now and a face-to-face encounter with a guy who should know something meaningful about the murder victim.

What next? Grace Academy would be locked up tight throughout the holiday weekend, so no point in stopping there in hopes of talking to someone today. That left Melissa Eldon's apartment complex.

David found the place—a three-story, redbrick structure sprawling over an acre of land. Each unit sported an air conditioner poking from the outside wall and a pint-size balcony. He was able to open the outermost door and enter a cubicle where the mailboxes filled one wall. He'd be surprised if the police hadn't been here to interview the manager and gain access to the victim's apartment, but M. Eldon still graced the label on mailbox number 212.

David tried the inner door, but it was locked. Typical. He pressed a button that was supposed to buzz the manager, but got no response. As he gazed helplessly through the window of the inner door, a thirtysomething woman came down the steps, trundling a baby on her hip and holding a toddler by the hand.

Brow wrinkled in inquiry, she came to the door. The infant snuggled close to her bosom, sucking her thumb and gazing at him with large eyes. The little boy fixed him with a skeptical stare as he clung to his mother's leg.

"Who are you looking for?" the woman asked through the glass.

"I was trying to buzz the manager," he answered.

"She's gone for the holiday. If you want an application, one can be downloaded online."

"Actually, I was going to ask her about a tenant here—Melissa Eldon."

The woman's tweezed brows climbed upward. "You a reporter?"

He shook his head and tried what he hoped was a nonchalant grin. "I'm an acquaintance of an acquaintance looking into what might have happened."

Her gaze narrowed, and then a sly smile formed on her lips. "A private investigator," she said as if delighted by her deduction. "Always wanted to meet one."

Denial sprang to David's lips, but his tongue refused to form the words. He wouldn't lie to her directly, but what could it hurt to let her think what she wanted?

"Mommy! Canny bar!" the toddler whined and tugged at the woman's jean-clad leg.

"Just a second, Austin." She glanced down, then

returned her attention to David and shrugged. "Guess I can tell you what I told the police. Miss Snip is—er, *was* my neighbor."

The woman's color heightened. "Sorry about speaking ill of the dead, but she wasn't easy to be around. Got annoyed with any of the kids in the building if they made noise or went a little fast in the halls. C'mon, kids are going to be kids! She was especially hard on my two if they laughed or cried too much, and she told me about it. Frequently. Even called the manager on us if our little dog yipped now and then. Quite a prima donna." She shook her head. "Made me wonder why she moved into this family-oriented apartment complex."

"Logical question," David said. "Do you have any idea where she was from?"

"Not a clue…" Her lips pursed. "I just remembered. Didn't even tell the police this. I should probably call them about it." Eagerness skimmed her expression.

"About what?"

The woman smirked. "I noticed Melissa wearing a college T-shirt one day when I ran into her in the laundry room."

"Which college?"

"Not sure. The shirt was baggy and faded. Some of the letters were worn off, and her long hair covered others. I made out the word *university,* and I remember a picture of an animal—some kind of fierce-looking cat. I didn't bother asking. She always thought she was too good to make small talk with the likes of me, unless she wanted to make some more complaints."

David's heart sank. The number of colleges and universities with feline mascots were legion.

The toddler started to whine again, and David lifted his hand in farewell. "Thanks a lot. You've been very helpful. Have a nice day."

"You, too." She transferred her attention to her offspring. "Yes, Austin, we're going to the vending machine now."

The trio drifted away from the door, and David went outside to his SUV, wearing a frown.

A teacher who didn't like kids or pets. That was red-flag weird, especially since she'd gotten engaged to someone with a son. Did Gil's money make up for having to deal with a stepchild? Did she take a job at an exclusive school in the first place in order to have access to the well-to-do parents? An intelligent beauty looking to make a match with a monied man was an old, old story. These factors made an unsavory combination with potential to have bearing on the reason she was dead.

Gil just went to the top of David's suspect list. It didn't sound as if she was the type of woman to marry for love. Was she two-timing her fiancé, and he found out about it? Or had he just discovered that she only wanted him for his money? The problem was David couldn't envision Gil with the gumption to do anything about the betrayal except sob into his snifter. At the symposium it had become clear that he was a silver-spoon sort of guy who'd spent no effort in accumulating the wealth he'd inherited. David's wealth came through inheritance, too, but he hadn't grown up in the lap of anything approaching luxury.

As he climbed into the vehicle, his phone began to play Pachelbel's *Canon in D*. It was Chris. Finally.

"Hey, buddy," David answered. "Who got their wish?"

Chris's chuckle warmed his ear. "I did…and she did."

"How does that work?"

"Little Samuel is perfect from the top of his fuzzy head to the tips of his pudgy toes. I hope someday you'll get the chance to know exactly what I'm saying, but the second you hold that new life in your arms, gender ceases to matter. You simply can't imagine the little person being anyone else except who they turned out to be."

"That makes sense."

"Sammy got a little stubborn right in the middle of things and took his sweet time getting born. We were up all night. I'm on my way back to the hospital after catching forty winks. I've only got a few minutes to yak, so update me fast on the status of your investigation."

David shared what little he'd learned.

Chris clucked his tongue. "I like the lead on the fiancé. Definitely talk to him. The lead on the university has some promise. One of the most common times for a young adult to get a tattoo is in college."

David frowned. "Alicia told me she went to the University of Texas at San Antonio, but only for a couple of years before she dropped out. Their mascot is a longhorn steer, not some kind of cat."

Chris made a humming sound. "It's still possible that Alicia and Melissa knew each other when they were in college. San Antonio has a couple of colleges—they could have gone to different schools but still become friends. You said yourself that Alicia dropped out. Melissa may have transferred to a school with a cat mascot or even have held a graduate degree from a different institution."

"I see what you mean. I'll pursue that angle. We keep coming back to the need to know more about her, and I won't have access until Friday to the person who might know."

"You could fly to San Antonio and spend Thanksgiving with our little fam. It's likely to be take-out turkey dinner, but hey, you probably weren't going to have anything different anyway. At least you'd have company eating it."

Chris sounded genuine about the invitation, but David would feel like the biggest heel on the planet for inserting himself into this family newly bonding with one another.

"Nah, I'll hang around here to catch any developments. The news of the murder could break to the public at any second. Actually, I forgot to listen to the noon report, so I should check the news services right now."

"Do that, pal. Good luck. I'm just walking into the hospital. I've got to go make like a daddy. It can be a dirty job, especially when Maddie insists it's my turn to change the diaper, but somebody has to do it." He laughed, and David laughed with him despite a sour twist in his gut.

"Good luck back at you, buddy," he said and ended the call.

David sat scowling at his phone. What kind of a rotten dude was suddenly jealous of a guy changing dirty diapers? That useless wishing-for-a-family thing again.

The outdoor chill began to dominate the interior of his Lexus, and he started the vehicle. He tapped his phone to access his news apps, but Pachelbel began to play again. Laurel! He answered quickly.

"David here."

"Mr. Greene?" Caroline's breathless voice responded.

David's stomach clenched. "Are you and your mom all right?"

"We're fine, except Mom's about to pop over all the news reporters calling the house phone or ringing the doorbell."

"The news broke, then."

"Ya think? Mom's been saying no comment, but the reporters aren't happy about it, and they're persistent. Finally, we sneaked out the rear door and went back to Janice's, so I guess the cleanup work is done for the day."

"Is there anything I can do to help?"

"Not with the reporters—I only brought them up because I knew you'd totally get it. You've been there, too. No, I called because I was just in Janice's fridge after a soda and saw this ginormous turkey thawing in there. That bird's way too big for the three of us to eat so…" The girl's voice trailed away.

David's heart warmed, but he'd better err on the side of caution. "If you're issuing an invitation, you should clear that idea with the adults first."

"I know, but before I hit them up I wanted to ask you something."

"Shoot."

"Do you know how to cook a turkey? I mean Mom and Janice will do their best and mean well, but I have yet to eat one of their Thanksgiving turkeys that didn't taste like gluey paper."

"The secret is in the seasoning, how long you cook the bird and at what temperature."

"You *do* know how to cook a turkey."

David fell silent as images from childhood Thanksgivings filled his senses with memories of sights, sounds, tastes and smells. "It's been years, but I used to help my mom prepare the feast. Her cornbread and apple stuffing could have won awards."

"Yum! You have got to come tomorrow and rescue my taste buds from torture. I won't take no for an answer."

"Whoa, squirt. They have to agree—"

"Not from you. From *them!* Keep your phone on you. I'll call you back."

The connection went silent. David lowered his cell, chuckling. Should he hope the invitation came through? The prospect of a real Thanksgiving dinner in an atmosphere approximating family appealed to him like a siren's song. And besides, Caroline was right—he *did* know what they were going through with the reporters, and he wanted to be there for them in the struggle. He wasn't objective about Laurel and Caroline any longer, and that was dangerous. Was continued association with them setting his heart up for shipwreck?

TEN

Today was Thanksgiving Day, and Laurel was going to be thankful if it killed her. Sometimes a thankful heart was a decision, not an emotion. She sank onto a stool and stared at the raw turkey perched on the center island of Janice's kitchen. At least she didn't have to worry about dressing the bird this holiday. Caroline had engineered a solution to that issue.

Laurel would laugh about her daughter's transparent manipulation to get David invited to their Thanksgiving dinner if she wasn't so conflicted about his presence in their lives. She liked him, and that was dangerous. With this mutual suspicion like a wall of bars between them, there was no future in getting to know one another.

Yet she hadn't been able to resist Caroline's plea. Even Janice had taken her daughter's side, arguing that it was hardly Christ-like to leave the man to spend Thanksgiving Day all alone. Laurel had folded in the face of her daughter's desire for a delicious Thanksgiving feast—for once—combined with the Good Samaritan appeal.

The doorbell sounded, and Laurel rose from the stool. David was here. She smoothed the front of the azure-blue skirt and frilly white blouse she'd donned for the special day and patted her hair. Was her lipstick okay? Too late to check now.

She headed for the front door, but Caroline darted from the living room, and reached it ahead of her. The girl delivered a boisterous welcome to their guest, bubbling with teenage giggles. Laurel smiled, spirits buoyed by her daughter's happiness.

"Hi," David said. He cradled a small sack of groceries in one arm even as he extended a tub of deli fruit salad toward Laurel. "Thanks for inviting me."

As she accepted the tub, her gaze met and locked with his twinkling gray eyes, and a warm shiver flowed down her spine. This was going to be a wonderful day, and for a small window of time, she would throw caution to the winds and allow herself to enjoy the moment. What could it hurt?

Janice hustled out of her home office and added her greeting to the mix. Then they adjourned to her spacious kitchen and got about their appointed tasks amidst a flow of casual banter. No heavy topics allowed today, Janice decreed, and no one objected.

While David stuffed and basted the turkey with ingredients he'd brought along, Laurel peeled potatoes and placed them in a pot of water on the stove to be turned on later when the turkey was closer to being done. Janice whipped up a simple green bean casserole to be popped into the oven at the proper time, and Caroline put together a raw veggie tray. Dessert was already sitting on the kitchen counter, a pumpkin pie and a pecan pie, courtesy of the local bakery.

By noon, the aromas wafting through the house drew an audible growl from Laurel's stomach as she set the dining room table. Another stomach echoed the growl, and she turned to run smack into David. They jumped apart, gazes falling to their own middles, and laughed.

"Good thing the turkey is ready to come out," he said, "or I might start making serious inroads on the veggies. I think I might anyway." He grabbed a carrot stick from the tray that already graced the table, then headed for the kitchen.

"I'm with you." Laurel snatched a celery stick and followed him.

In short order, they sat around the table, the steaming feast before them. As casually as if this were an everyday event, David extended his hands to either side of him, and Laurel placed her palm in his. His fingers were firm around hers—strong and comforting, if she'd allow herself to think that way. Caroline joined her hand with David's. Frowning slightly, Janice took Laurel's and Caroline's hands. David's words of thanks were simple, but eloquent and heartfelt. Laurel had no problem adding her amen.

Then they dug in. David's turkey and dressing were gourmet quality. The turkey practically melted on the tongue, and the dressing demanded to be savored with every bite. In contrast, her mashed potatoes were a little on the watery side, and her gravy sported a few lumps, but not a soul uttered a word of complaint or criticism. Janice's green bean casserole erred on the salty side but it was edible, and the serving dishes were quickly depleted by hungry souls.

Laurel's heart sang. When had she last felt so relaxed? And right in the middle of the worst trouble she'd been in since Steven rolled through her life like a human wrecking ball.

"Anyone ready for pie?" Janice asked, rising from the table.

A chorus of groans answered her.

She laughed. "We can do pie later, then. Let's adjourn to the family room. I'll get a blaze going in the fireplace."

"Allow me." David raised a hand.

"Have at it. I'll brew some tea."

"All ri-i-ight!" Caroline smacked her hands together.

Soon snaps and crackles and pleasing warmth issued from the fireplace. Janice emerged from the kitchen bearing a tray of steaming mugs. Swathed in the comfort of an easy chair, Laurel accepted her mug and inhaled the brisk, fruity steam.

Engrossed in a fashion magazine, Caroline accepted her mug with scarcely a glance and a murmur of thanks. From a casual stance next to the mantelpiece, David lifted his mug in salute to the server and turned toward the colorful framed butterflies and moths on the mantel.

"Did you collect these or purchase them?" he asked Janice.

"My late husband collected and mounted them."

"They're beautiful. I'm sorry to hear he passed away. How long ago?"

"Eight years last month. Aneurism. No warning."

"That's tough."

"Yes, but at least Laurel and Caroline were around to prop me up until I got my bearings again." A shadow flitted across Janice's fine-boned features.

Laurel rose and laid a hand on her friend's shoulder. "There's been a lot of mutual propping going on over the years. Karl was a good guy. Even though we only knew him a few months before he passed, I miss him."

"Me, too," said Caroline, lifting her head from the magazine. "He took us all on one of his butterfly treks into the mountains. I was only five, but I still remember. It was fun."

Janice smiled. "Well, folks, if you can spare me for a little while, I have a couple of things to finish in the office, and then I'll dish the pie."

She disappeared up the hallway and then Caroline jumped up. "I'm supposed to Skype with Emily in a few minutes so I'll be upstairs."

Just like that, Laurel and David were abandoned in the family room. Her gaze met David's. He shrugged, smiled and took a seat in the easy chair opposite the one she'd claimed. She should feel awkward alone with this stranger who was becoming less of an outsider by the minute, but she didn't.

"Janice and Karl didn't have any children, I take it." David sipped from his mug, peering at her above the rim.

Laurel shook her head. "They were newlyweds when they moved in next to us."

"Really! That makes her widowhood doubly difficult. The honeymoon hadn't worn off."

"Janice hasn't had an easy road. Her first marriage was a nightmare from start to finish—one of the reasons we've bonded so tightly. Based on kindred experiences, we get each other."

"Kindred experiences like divorce or widowhood?"

"The nightmare marriage and divorce thing."

David studied the interior of his mug. "If you don't mind my asking, is Caroline's dad in the picture at all?" He settled a steady look on her.

"Her father is dead." Laurel summoned all her self-control to make that statement slowly and evenly. Funny how digging up thoughts of Steven still made her breathing go shallow and unsteady.

"But I thought you said—"

Laurel lifted a forestalling hand.

"Sorry." David's gaze dropped. "None of my business."

"It isn't, but it's not a secret either." She smiled to soften her words. "Steven Latrain left me for another woman more compliant and worshipful than I turned out to be, and I was grateful—both for Caroline's sake and for mine."

David sat forward. "Latrain? A member of the LTR banking family?"

"The very same. No one had ever said no to the boy, and at least to start with, I was no exception to the rule." She wrinkled her nose. "Actually, he was well into manhood when I met him—a good decade older than this nineteen-year-old, starry-eyed college freshman. He swept me off my feet, sometimes literally. Said all the right things. Steven was a classic narcissist. Doted on himself 24/7, but he had all the moves to make you feel like serving his every whim was the height of honor and privilege. Made me feel like a princess, which was quite something for a girl raised in a backwater Colorado village by a factory worker daddy who drank himself to death by the time I was Caroline's age."

"And your mother?"

"She was out of my life before I was six. Ran off with a golf celebrity. We never heard from her again as far as I know."

"That's sad."

"It still hurts, and I wonder sometimes, but I don't waste a lot of effort at it."

"I admire your strength and dedication in raising Caroline." David pursed his lips and sat back. "But the person I'm really sad for is the woman who missed out on the treasure of watching you grow up and enjoying an awesome granddaughter like Caroline."

Laurel caught her breath. "I—I hadn't thought of the matter in quite that light before. Thank you." Something within her heart unfurled like a flower receiving sunlight.

"Who cared for you after your father passed away? Some other relative?"

She snorted a laugh. "No one wanted me. I finished my underage years in a foster home. Not a bad one like you hear about—but not a real family either."

A scowl passed over David's face. "Sounds to me like Latrain preyed on a young woman who was vulnerable and hungry for promises of love and family."

"You said a mouthful. He should have picked up on the signal that I wasn't going to remain compliant forever when I insisted on vows and a ring before he could get everything he wanted from me. My mistake. I should have run the other way as fast as my legs could carry me. When Caroline was born, I began to develop independent thoughts. Big no-no in Steven's world. Let's just say…things got ugly real fast."

Laurel grimaced at the tea grown cold in her mug and set it aside.

"He was abusive?" David's face darkened, and fire flashed deep in those rain-swept eyes.

He didn't look like a man who could hurt a woman, but he sure looked like a man who could hurt a man who would hurt a woman. A silent thrill swept through her, but she resisted the sensation and turned her gaze toward the coffered ceiling.

"Not at first. The moment I met Steven, he began manipulating me mentally and emotionally, only I was too naive to know it. The more I wised up and began to break free, the more the abuse escalated to include mind and spirit and eventually body." She lifted her head and stared at David. "Some contrariness in my makeup wouldn't allow me to give in or back down. If something in his makeup hadn't made him distractible by easier prey, I could well be dead now. Sometimes I thought I was going to be. If not for Caroline, sometimes I wanted to be."

The angles and planes of David's face softened. "That's why you grabbed a weapon when a man you didn't know or trust came in from prowling outside in the middle of the night."

"I fool myself most of the time that I'm over the past, that I've put those defensive reactions to rest." She rubbed the bridge of her nose with two fingers. "But then I do something dumb on instinct like pull a knife on a guy going after firewood for his own fireplace in his own home."

"Not dumb." He reached across the distance that separated them and cradled one of her hands in his. "You, Laurel Adams, are one of the bravest, finest women I've ever met."

Laurel left her hand in his. For now. The moment wouldn't last long. He wouldn't want to hold her hand if he knew what she was really like, and she should tell him because she shouldn't want to hold his hand either. A relationship between them couldn't work.

"Not so brave. Not so fine." She met his gentle gaze and almost bit back the words that would condemn her, but the truth would put the necessary distance between them.

"When Steven divorced me to marry his next acolyte, he vowed that when he got back from his honeymoon, he was going to take Caroline away from me. He had the money and connections to pull it off, even though he didn't want her any more than he wanted me. He just needed to hurt me, and Caroline was a tool to do that.

"I was petrified. The day I was told that he'd fallen off his yacht and drowned, I was relieved. More than relieved. I didn't care that the new bride got everything that might have been of financial help to me or Caroline. She was welcome to it all!" Laurel leaned closer to him. "God forgive me, David, but I was fiercely glad he was gone and couldn't hurt Caroline, or me, or anyone else ever again."

Far from withdrawing his grip, David's fingers tightened around hers. "I'm glad, too. Not that Steven Latrain apparently died in a lost state in the eternal sense. I don't believe you're glad about that either. But I don't feel guilty for being thankful that you and Caroline were spared more of his poison. There's nothing wrong with that perspective. You were *not* responsible for his death."

"No, but—"

"No buts."

Why did this man's words and ways seem to break up stony ground in her heart? Tears stung her eyes, and a fat droplet trailed down her nose. If she didn't get herself under control, her eyes were going to turn red and puffy. How attractive. She sat back, reclaiming her hand, and wiped at her face.

"What are you saying to make my best friend cry?" The feminine growl came from the family room doorway.

Laurel gasped and turned her head. Janice stood, hands on hips, gaze narrowed on David. If she was a storm cloud, lightning was about to strike.

If glares were guns, no doubt he'd be dead right now. David spread his hands and opened his mouth, but Laurel jumped up and stood between him and her friend. David pressed his lips together. It bruised his ego that she didn't seem to think he could take care of himself…but judging from the look on Janice's face, maybe it was better if Laurel handled this.

"Down, girlfriend," Laurel said in a half placating, half teasing tone. "Tears can be good, you know. These were."

Janice harrumphed.

David stepped around Laurel. "It's been refreshing to enjoy a homemade Thanksgiving dinner, I'm honored you included me in your company today, but I have a few things on my plate that I need to accomplish, so I'll leave you folks to a relaxing afternoon."

"Don't go, David." Laurel's hand closed around his arm. "We haven't had our pie yet."

Her pleading gaze pierced his resolve, but he steeled himself. What had he been thinking going all soft with Laurel when he knew how bleak their prospects were? He shouldn't have accepted the invitation today, nor should he have pried into her past. Janice's cold water on an intimate moment had done them both a favor.

He patted his stomach. "I'm still full to the brim."

"I'll put a piece in a to-go container," Janice said.

"Don't…bother." David's voice trailed away because the woman had already disappeared.

Laurel walked him to the door, somber faced. "Don't mind Janice. She's protective."

"No worries. I get it." He sent her a half smile.

"Caroline," Laurel called up the stairs as he shrugged into his jacket. "Our guest is leaving."

"Already?" A tattoo of running feet punctuated the cry.

Caroline barreled down the stairs and flung her arms around David. He hugged her back, heart aching. This kid deserved a good daddy to go with her fine mama.

"Thanks for coming," the girl said. "The turkey and dressing were awesome. I wish you didn't have to go so soon. I'm done talking to Emily. If Janice had a piano, we could do a concert together, but maybe you could stay for a quick game of Scrabble."

"Another time, squirt." He tweaked her chin. *God, help me keep that promise.*

"Here you go." Janice thrust a sealed container toward him. Her gaze had softened, but it was still firm.

"Thanks." He dipped his chin toward her. "I appreciate the hospitality."

Grim amusement lit her green eyes. "You're welcome."

She didn't add *now get lost,* but he took the hint when she opened the door for him.

"Janice!" Laurel's soft hiss reached his ears as the door shut behind him.

He'd be amused about Laurel's exasperation with her friend if he didn't agree with the woman's take on the situation. Apparently, she had the sense to see that the attraction between him and Laurel, as well as Caroline's fixation on him, was headed toward nothing but hurt.

No doubt she regretted inviting him, but he couldn't feel that way. The sense of belonging, even if only for a few hours, had rejuvenated his spirit. And his purpose. It was time for answers so he could clear the Adamses' names, and find the killer once and for all. His meeting with Gilbert Montel tomorrow couldn't come quickly enough.

ELEVEN

With a long sigh, Laurel flung herself backward onto her bed. *Her* bed. Finally!

A contractor had surprised her Thanksgiving evening by calling to say he could come fix that door and change those locks the next day after all. Laurel had been over here early to let them in and then retired to her own room in order to stay out of the workers' hair.

From sounds below, the job was well under way. Tonight she and Caroline could spend their first night home after a seeming eternity of absence. Only a few days had passed, but so much had happened—was still happening. At least the problems might seem more bearable in their own home.

Things had gotten a bit strained at Janice's house after she'd shooed David away. Not that her friend hadn't done Laurel a favor. She was getting way too comfortable with a man who she'd be wise to keep at arm's length. Growing closer to David was the last thing she needed…no matter what Caroline seemed to think.

Why did you urge me to agree to invite him to Thanksgiving dinner? she'd demanded of Janice after David left.

Her friend had shrugged and nodded toward Caroline. *You know I'm putty in your daughter's hands. What she wanted I made sure she got. I didn't think you two would get so chummy. Besides, I told Caroline to make sure never to leave you alone in the same room.*

I didn't promise! Caroline had lifted her chin.

Laurel had laughed and wagged a finger at Janice. *I think both of us have been royally scammed by a teenage matchmaker.*

You like David. I know you do. Caroline had fixed big eyes on her mother.

Laurel had wrapped her daughter in a one-armed hug. *You like him, too, but now isn't the best time to get close to someone like that.*

Caroline had broken away from the embrace. *Someone like what? He's a good guy. You find fault with any man who comes into your life. But here you meet a real-life champion of the underdog, and you push him away.*

A what? Laurel had gaped.

Caroline had rolled her eyes. *Don't you get it? He didn't ask for our brand of trouble. We got dumped on his doorstep, complete with a dead body. Remember? But he's stuck by us and given us the benefit of the doubt every step. You don't meet a person like that every day.*

She'd stomped up the stairs.

What's this about "a man like that?" Janice's brow had creased. *Is there some reason, other than my chronic best-friend overprotectiveness, that I shouldn't want you to get close to David Greene?*

Don't you recognize him?

Janice had shaken her head. *I assume he's got money—poor men don't drive Lexuses, or hire security details at the drop of a hat. But you and I are both wary of rich guys—for good reason.*

Three years ago, David's mug was all over the news in connection with his girlfriend's murder. He was never brought to trial.

Janice's lips had formed an *O* to match her eyes. *Was that during the six months I was abroad learning international realty practice?*

Laurel had smacked her forehead. *Of course! Between your absence from the country and your general disgust for network news, I suppose you never were exposed to that media frenzy.*

Another good reason to be wary, then, girlfriend. Janice had shaken her head. *Enough about David Greene. How about a game of Scrabble?*

Laurel had agreed to the game, but inside she'd moped the rest of Thanksgiving until the call from the contractor lifted her spirits a small degree. Now, with the sunshine of a new morning streaming through her bedroom window, she mulled over Caroline's stinging words.

While it was true that Laurel's minor forays into

dating over the years had never turned into anything that lasted, Caroline hadn't taken into account that her mother worked daily with real-life champions of the underdog. It wasn't Laurel's fault that nothing had developed between her and any of the single men at the office, was it? If there was no chemistry there was no chemistry. The spark wasn't something that could be conjured by decision.

But maybe it could be doused by decision. Had she built impregnable walls around her heart?

Laurel rolled onto her side. The theory wasn't holding water right now. She wasn't having much luck toning down her attraction to David. Caroline had been perceptive enough to notice. Janice, too.

Laurel also had to admit her daughter was spot-on that she was hypercautious in relationships. She had good reasons—reasons she planned never to expose to her daughter. What kid needed to deal with the reality that her father not only walked out on her mother and on her, but had been a selfish, manipulative, violent man who she was lucky never to have known beyond her earliest years?

Why had she told David about the ugly past history? Maybe because she'd made herself vulnerable by deciding to relax and go with the flow yesterday, and David had been such an understanding ear.

Another question nagged—why was he so interested in everything about them? Her caution meter was registering an ulterior motive in David's unexplained loyalty to a pair of strangers who'd dragged him into contact with another murder investigation. His willingness to hang around them didn't make sense, and her ego wasn't inflated enough to think he was championing them, as Caroline put it, because he found her irresistible.

She could be wrong to be so distrustful. It could be another one of those defensive instincts she'd discussed with David that was leading her astray. *Please God, let me be wrong.* But Laurel wasn't yet ready to abandon her doubts about David Greene.

David paced Gil Montel's office, where the housekeeper had ushered him to wait for his host. Afternoon sunlight invaded the vast room in muted stripes between half-drawn blinds. Finely woven oriental rugs covered large swatches of ebony-wood flooring, and neatly stuffed bookshelves coated the opposing walls not taken by the entrance door and the windows to the outside. The titles on the books' spines reflected a voracious and eclectic but rather dry taste in reading material.

By the neatly squared papers on the man's desk, the artwork and knickknacks positioned just so and the general lack of lived-in clutter, David deduced that Gil was either a fastidious soul, had a meticulous housekeeper or didn't spend much time in this room. The latter seemed unlikely as many of the decor items were personal in nature, the chair behind the desk showed traces of wear. Also, the air carried a hint of masculine cologne. An expensive brand.

A small table in the corner of the sprawling room bore a large photograph in a fancy frame. From a corner of the frame, a gold chain dangled, bearing a small, round pendant filigreed with the initials UTSA. Not likely to be a person's initials. Some sort of organization? The table was covered in midnight blue velvet, and the photo was surrounded by bric-a-brac like small but fancy candles, a string of pearls and a single silk rose blossom on a long stem. A shrine of sorts?

David studied the photo. A beaming Gil had his arm around a stunning brunette several inches taller than himself. Apparently this guy's taste ran to statuesque women. The brunette's expression was pleasant, but the muted smile seemed mildly derisive, as if she found the adoration of the man beside her a little ridiculous. Was this Gil's first wife?

When he and David had accidentally sat next to each other at the hotel bar after the financial symposium, Gil's wife's death from cancer less than a year prior had been part of the man's reason for tears. The other part had been the murder of his sister at the hands of her groom while on their honeymoon. That traumatic event had occurred only two weeks before the investor's conference. Clearly, the poor guy was in no shape to have attended the symposium, but maybe he'd needed the distraction.

At that time in his life, David had been self-centered and unsympathetic, absorbed in drowning his own pain in an excess of booze, drugs and babes. Alicia had been the latest in a long string of wild relationships, but with her he'd been just about ready to commit. That night, he'd been uncomfortable with Gil's gushing grief and grateful when Alicia showed up to drag him off to a dining table well away from the shattered man. Would his impression of Gilbert Montel change at this meeting?

"The photo is of my sister, Paula, and me," announced a high tenor voice David remembered from that evening in the bar.

He turned to find a portly, balding man on the short side of five foot seven staring at him from the doorway. Montel wore a pair of crisply creased slacks and tasseled brown loafers. Beneath a tan polo shirt, the man's spine was straight and his shoulders squared, but a trace of reddened puffiness around the eyes betrayed either lack of sleep or recent expressions of grief—or both.

"She was gorgeous," David responded.

"Indeed." He frowned. "Her blessing and her curse was to so closely resemble our mother. I, on the other hand, inherited my father's looks and dimensions. Not much blessing in that, though he left me other assets to compensate." A wry smile flickered.

David hadn't pictured Gil as a man capable of self-awareness, much less the ability to laugh at himself, and he was left speechless.

"You seem to catch me at stressful times in my

life," Gil said as he walked in and sat down behind the desk. He motioned David to a cushy leather guest chair. "Shall I call for a couple glasses of sherry?" He reached toward an intercom button on the corner of his desk.

"No, thanks anyway," David answered as he took the offered seat. "I won't stay long. I've been in Denver since two days before Thanksgiving and thought it only right to stop and offer my condolences. I read about your engagement and then saw the news about your fiancée on the television. What a terrible thing."

All true statements, just not the whole picture. David shushed his conscience. He was on an important mission.

Muscles in Gil's round cheeks twitched and his lips trembled but the moisture glistening in his eyes never pooled into tears. The man cleared his throat and looked away, blinking. "Thank you. I appreciate you taking the time to drop by. You have no idea what it meant to me that you allowed me to bend your ear with my troubles when we met at that symposium a few years back." Gil offered a weak smile.

David's gut twisted. Way to make him feel like the heel du jour. Good thing the guy hadn't been able to read his mind back then...or now. How could he pump this hurting man for information under false pretenses? He couldn't, that's how.

Yet how could he not? Wasn't it vital to solve these murders? Shouldn't discovering the significance of the mutual tattoos, if any, be a priority? All he wanted to do was find out if Alicia and Melissa knew each other. That information would be enough to take to the police, and he might at last be able to come clean with Laurel about his particular interest in Melissa Eldon's murder. What a relief that would be!

"Had you known Melissa long?" David crossed his legs in a posture of relaxation.

"We met in New York. Bumped into each other at a Broadway play we were attending and hit it off. She was looking for a teaching job. The only suitable position in Denver of which I was aware was at my son's school. I put in a good word for her, and she got the job. We took our relationship from there. Had we—" the man halted and cleared his throat "—had we married, she would have quit her job and found herself fully occupied with our social calendar. Melissa was a fabulous hostess and handled herself magnificently among the best people."

The best people? Oh, yes, the people with money, power and position. That Gil Montel was a snob came as no surprise. At least in part, Montel hadn't been marrying a woman; he'd been marrying an asset. Some of the sympathy he felt for the man's grief dissipated.

"I feel responsible." A choking sound followed Gil's words.

"For her death? Why, man?" David leaned forward.

Gil shook his head. "If I hadn't brought her to Denver, she might never have crossed the path of a killer."

"How do you know she came across her killer here?"

Gil's mouth fell open and then he shut it. "I guess I don't. Are you saying someone could have followed her here?"

"I'm saying that, at least from the information the police have released to the news services, no one knows yet. Did she skip out on a jealous boyfriend in New York?"

"No!" The man's nostrils flared.

David dropped his gaze. Touchy area for Mr. Montel. Too touchy. Perhaps where there was smoke... He offered Gil an apologetic smile. "Just trying to think like the police might think. I'm sure they're checking all the angles."

Gil sniffed. "At the risk of being indelicate, I would imagine the 'jealous boyfriend' scenario is at the forefront of your mind."

David's hands fisted, but he kept them below the edge of the desk. His supposed motive for murdering Alicia had been the role of jealous boyfriend. But he honestly hadn't known until after her death that there'd been any reason for jealousy. Alicia had been crafty in her activities outside of their relationship.

"Touché!" He kept his tone well modulated.

"Then we're even." Gil rose. "If you will excuse me, I have arrangements to finalize."

David stood. "Arrangements?"

"Funeral."

"What about Melissa's family?"

"None to speak of." Gil waved a hand.

"I'll take my leave, then." Spirits sinking, David followed Gil to the door of the study. Some sleuth he was. He'd discovered exactly nada. Asking the guy point blank about the tattoo had been out of the question, but at least he'd hoped to uncover some background information on the woman—like where she was raised or educated.

David headed for the front door and was met by the housekeeper, who handed him his jacket. As he shrugged into it, a colorful brochure on an antique refectory table caught his eye. Moran & Connor. Cremation. Burial. Pre-Planning. Live Well. Leave Well. Another piece of useless information. Or was it?

He paused as brisk November air welcomed him to the outdoors. Obituaries commonly listed details from the life of the deceased. If the arrangements were being finalized this afternoon, perhaps by this evening he might find an obituary published on the mortuary's website.

A smile tilted David's lips. Fresh anticipation flickered as he strode toward the cobblestone drive, where his SUV was hidden behind a hedge of tall shrubs. He stepped through the archway built into the hedge and collided with another body.

"Oooph!" The exclamation left David's lips as

he staggered backward. The young man he'd run into also staggered, but to the accompaniment of vivid profanity.

"Watch where you're going, dimbo." Gil's younger mirror image peered up at David. "Oh, I thought you were dad's dweeb of a chauffeur. Who are you?"

David frowned. This must be Grant, beloved and only offspring of the lord of the manor. The kid's facial features were his father's, but his body build was lean like his murdered aunt's.

"I'm an acquaintance of your father's here to offer condolences," David said. "You have my sympathy also. It must be hard to believe you might be getting a mother and then to have her snatched away under such awful circumstances."

"Ms. Eldon?" Grant's face reddened as he snorted and called the woman a foul name. "She was never going to be my mother."

The young man barged around him and disappeared up the walk. A chill swept over David that had nothing to do with the fall weather.

Didn't Laurel mention that the breath of the prowler who knocked her into the bushes several days ago smelled of nacho chips? David had caught a whiff of the same on Grant's breath, and the boy's height and build fit the rest of the description Laurel had given, too.

And hadn't Gil said he'd gotten Melissa Eldon a job at the school where his son attended? Since a penchant for nacho chips wasn't exactly uncommon among teenagers, David's hunch wasn't iron-clad, but Grant could be the rich man's son who was pestering Caroline to go out with him. Gil certainly fit the criteria of someone who could virtually fund a private school.

This encounter with Grant Montel revealed the boy as bitter, angry and arrogant. If he really was the one Caroline had described, then no wonder she didn't want to hang around with him. The girl had good sense and better taste. But no surprise that she was intimidated by the situation. Even though David's deduction was unverified, he couldn't keep silent. Grant Montel was potentially dangerous.

Dangerous enough to kill his teacher in order to prevent her from becoming his stepmother? Vengeful enough to dump her body where suspicion would fall on the girl who'd spurned his interest? Maybe he was leaping to conclusions, but he wanted to share this information with Laurel. Her and Caroline's safety was at stake. If there was a chance that Grant was involved, then who knew what the kid might pull next?

Darkness settled over David's spirits even as he buckled himself into the driver's seat of his SUV. If Grant was the culprit, what became of his hopes that the victims were connected by the tattoos in a manner that led to their deaths? Hope evaporated, that's what.

But if this hunch panned out then, while he might have to go on living under the onus of suspicion,

Laurel and Caroline would be free. He would have to find comfort in that knowledge and disappear from their lives forever. His insides went numb. The pain would come later.

No one answered the door at Janice's house, but a contractor's van parked at the curb gave David a clue that Laurel and Caroline might have gone home. He went next door, and Laurel answered the doorbell. Her smile held warmth, as if she might be glad to see him.

"Has Caroline spoken with you about an issue with a boy at school?" he asked without preamble.

The smile faded and she nodded. "She's offered a little information. I'm on hold for more."

"I think we need to pin her down now. I've just had a disturbing encounter."

Eyes widening, Laurel motioned him inside and called for Caroline. The girl trotted into the foyer. Her eyes lit up when they landed on him, but then her expression sobered as she gazed from him to her mother and back again.

"What's up?"

"Is Grant Montel the young man who's been bothering you at school?" he asked.

Caroline's gaze fell to her toes. Silence spoke louder than the noise of a drill deeper inside the house. Slowly, Caroline nodded.

David looked toward Laurel. "Your daughter hasn't exaggerated this kid's creepiness. And he's got nacho breath."

Laurel's mouth formed an *O* as color receded from her face. "He was the one outside our house, the one who knocked me over? He's been *stalking* her?"

"It's possible."

Caroline sniffled. "I didn't *do* anything to make him like me."

Laurel embraced her daughter. "It's not your fault, sweetheart." Her tone was fierce.

She gazed at David across her daughter's shoulder. "Thank you for sharing this with us. I *am* going to take the matter to the police. I don't care how much money his daddy has, or even if I have to pull Caroline out of that school."

"Good decision." David nodded. "You might be interested to know Grant didn't like Ms. Eldon any better than your daughter did, and his father was getting ready to marry her."

Laurel inhaled a sharp breath and released Caroline. "She was engaged? I didn't notice a ring on her finger when we found the body, but then I wasn't coherent enough to take in details."

"She had one," Caroline spoke up. "Got it the week before Thanksgiving vacation. A great big rock, and she flaunted it. Stared at it for minutes at a time—like it was some crystal ball—while we worked on assignments. I told you she was a head case, Mom."

"How come you didn't tell me your teacher was engaged?"

"I was afraid if I started talking about Ms. Eldon and Mr. Montel, I'd get carried away, and the whole mess with his son liking me would come out. I knew how much it meant to you for me to attend that school. If I told you what was going on and you made a fuss, I was the one more likely to get expelled than Grant Montel. Besides, a guy with Mr. Montel's influence could make trouble for you and SPC. He's one of your best contributors, right?"

Laurel groaned. "Honey, I'm glad I raised a thoughtful daughter, but I'm sorry I made you leery of standing up to bullies with money and power. The opposite was my intention."

"I'm not scared to stand up to them. I turned Grant down, didn't I?"

"You certainly did. I'm proud of your good sense."

Caroline beamed. "I kept hoping he'd develop a crush on someone else. Maybe over the holiday break he'd—"

"A crush is one thing," David said. "Stalking is quite another."

He refrained from adding the possibility of murder to eliminate the threat of an unwanted stepmother. Laurel's knowing gaze met his. She was under no illusion as to what this scenario might mean. Perhaps the police already knew about Grant's dislike for his father's fiancée, but providing motive for the young man to place her body in Laurel's trunk might spur a deeper investigation.

"Thank you, David, for bringing all this to our

attention. How did you happen to find these things out?"

He summarized his brief history with Gilbert Montel, and his conversations at the man's house today.

"Can you stay for supper?" Laurel asked when he finished. Her eyes gleamed gratitude.

If only she knew how deeply her invitation tempted him, but continued interaction could only lead to more pain later—for him anyway—when the inevitable goodbye-for-good needed to be said. Best he say it now.

"I can't. I need to head home to Texas."

Caroline made a sound of disappointment.

The light in Laurel's eyes faded. "Tonight?"

"As soon as possible."

"I see. We've kept you in Denver long enough. We appreciate everything you've done for us. Don't we, Caroline?"

"Sure, Mr. Greene. Are you coming back soon?"

Laurel gave her daughter The Look, and Caroline subsided with a frown.

David's heart tore, but he pasted on a smile. "I can't say I have immediate plans to return to Denver, squirt, but you never know." He offered a breezy wave and stepped onto the porch.

Laurel followed, hugging herself against the chill. "Just a minute, David. Please send me the bill for the man from the security service. I noticed he was outside in the van again last night. You can call him off now. We're in our own home, the locks are being changed as we speak and the home security system will be upgraded early next week."

"I could have him stand down, but don't give the bill a second thought. The whole thing was my idea anyway."

"But—"

David lifted a hand to forestall the protest. "It's been great to know you." How heartfelt those words were he could never let her guess. "You'd better get back inside now before you turn into an icicle."

"Goodbye, David. Thanks again."

Was he mistaken, or did pain shadow her expressive brown eyes? He'd never know, and he couldn't afford to torment himself with the question.

David drove back to his hotel, taking a small detour through a fast-food drive-through. In his room, he picked at the burger and fries. He really wasn't in a big hurry to face the long drive back to Texas. He'd probably take off in the morning.

His lead with the Montel boy looked promising, but it wasn't a sure thing. Until an arrest was made, Laurel would have to be okay with him not calling off the personal bodyguard during the nighttime hours. Maybe she'd get riled enough to call him and chew on his ear. David smiled at the prospect of talking to her again.

Of course, he could be talking to her now if he'd accepted the offer to stay for dinner. He knew he'd made the right decision, but the night ahead of him stretched out long and empty.

He logged in to his computer, eager to find something to occupy his thoughts. Might as well check out that obituary for Melissa Eldon.

Ten minutes later, he was tossing things willy-nilly into his suitcase and talking on the phone with the night-duty receptionist at an air charter business at the same time. Forget driving back to Texas. He was flying to San Antonio on a private plane as quickly as one could be gassed up and ready.

Ms. Eldon got her master's degree in biology from Villanova University of Philadelphia, hence the wildcat emblem on the T-shirt her apartment neighbor had spotted. But she received her Bachelor of Science degree from the University of Texas at San Antonio. The year of graduation would have put Melissa there as a freshman the same year as Alicia.

Did that mean the women had known each other? Maybe, maybe not. And even if they had known each other and shared a taste in tattoo designs, the convergence of their lives didn't mean their murders were related.

But it didn't mean they weren't.

TWELVE

"What do you mean this information is irrelevant to the murder investigation?" Laurel demanded of Detective Iceberg, as she'd mentally dubbed him. Her lawyer laid a hand on her arm, and she subsided.

It was Monday morning following the Thanksgiving holiday, and she perched on the edge of an uncomfortable chair across from the detective in a conference room at the police station. Darren Chantler, her lawyer, sat on one side of her and Caroline on the other. She'd hated to expose her daughter to this stress, but she'd assumed the police would need her daughter's statement in regard to Grant's behavior. The sterile cubicle of bare gray walls, dull linoleum floor and timeworn table meshed with the odor of stale sweat in a way that set Laurel's teeth on edge. The environment was probably planned with that effect in mind.

Berg's impassive blue eyes didn't blink before her outrage. "We were aware that Grant Montel didn't favor his father's remarriage. That's not an uncommon attitude among children of another parent. However, when we investigated his whereabouts at the time the victim was killed, we eliminated him as a suspect. He was out of town at a relative's, a fact that we have verified."

Laurel's insides deflated, and Caroline let out a small whimper.

Chantler hummed. "Perhaps that is the case, but apparently young Mr. Montel has been harassing and stalking one of my clients. That allegation is hardly irrelevant."

Berg frowned. "The police department takes stalking seriously. I'll refer you to an officer who investigates such charges. She'll take the young lady's statement." The detective rose.

"When exactly *did* Ms. Eldon die?" The question spurted from Laurel's lips, and her lawyer shot her an alarmed stare. She ignored him. "And where? She certainly didn't expire in my trunk. And how? If I'd done it, I'd know the answers to all these questions, but I don't."

Berg regarded her soberly. "How do you think she died?"

"Don't answer that," Chantler said briskly.

But Laurel rose and leaned toward the detective. "If you think my mind has been playing with all sorts of scenarios of what could have happened to the woman, you'd be right. That's normal for anyone thrust into a horrifying situation and left to cope without a scrap of information that could dispel confusion and fear. I don't appreciate being stonewalled and treated like a suspect when I know—I *know*—that Caroline and I are victims."

A smile formed on the detective's lips. "You're good. I can see why you make a fine living as a public speaker." He left the room and closed the door behind him.

"You go, Mom!" Caroline pumped a fist.

At the moment, Laurel wouldn't have minded planting one of those squarely on Detective Iceberg's smug grin. She urgently needed to get a leash on her emotions. But how? The promise of another suspect for the police to consider had turned out bankrupt. Hot air gushed through her nose as she sank into her seat.

Chantler, a petite middle-aged man with shrewd hazel eyes, regarded her kindly. "I agree with your daughter. You expressed yourself well, but you would do better to allow me to deal with the authorities."

"But they're convinced we're guilty."

The lawyer pursed his lips. "Perhaps. Or perhaps they're still fishing. One thing I know, if they had sufficient proof, you wouldn't be free to walk out of here after Caroline gives her statement."

"At least there's that silver lining."

David had brought them what he thought was a ray of hope. Now that hope was gone—and so was he. She and Caroline were on their own. Isn't that how she'd lived her life until now? Why wasn't she pleased to return to status quo? Her heart whispered answers that her mind refused to hear.

An hour later, they left the police station. Their lawyer took off in his little blue sports car, and Laurel and Caroline settled into the rental they'd been using since last Friday.

"Mo-o-om, I don't want to go to school today." Caroline slumped in her seat. "Grant will be there, and all the kids will have heard about Ms. Eldon being found in our trunk. I don't think I can handle the stares and the whispers and the questions."

"I know how you feel, honey." Laurel started the car. "Walter wants me to sit this week out of the office and work from home. Give the media attention time to die down." So far, such phone calls and doorbell rings had been answered with no comment, and the calls had diminished considerably already. "How about I have the school send your work home for this week, and then next week we can both return to business as usual with our heads held high?"

"You rock, Mom!" Caroline grinned, and Laurel's spirits lifted.

The day dragged by as if each hour wore a ball and chain. Laurel attempted to accomplish paperwork online, but couldn't concentrate properly. Caroline stuck to her room for most of the day, but showed up at Laurel's office door toward the end of the afternoon.

"Could we call David and ask if he knows someone who can clean the piano keyboard? It's still full of dried goop."

Laurel sent her a sympathetic smile. After the fiasco with the police this morning, she'd had a tough time not punching in a certain number on her phone also. But their problems shouldn't be David's, and she wouldn't burden him when he clearly wanted to return to his own life.

"We don't need to call David for that. He's not from the Denver area. Do some research for me online or in the Yellow Pages, okay? We can make contacts ourselves."

Caroline nodded and wandered away, shoulders drooping. Laurel's throat tightened, but she pushed away the threat of tears. Heartache had visited her many times before, but had eventually packed its bags and slunk out the door. She had to believe this visit would prove temporary also.

But what if she or Caroline, or both of them, ended up behind bars? Could she bear that?

Eyes closed, she bowed her head. "God, we're in Your hands. I can only cling to trust that You're at work to save us."

She didn't add the obvious—that she saw no evidence of such grace operating in the situation. Over the years she'd noticed how frequently God worked in secret until the eleventh hour. There were times— like now—when Laurel wished it weren't so, but faith often had to be blind.

* * *

"Nope. Sorry, I've never done a tat like that. Or seen one either." From the opposite side of a sales counter, a grizzled tattoo artist shook his head at the smartphone photo David was showing him.

"Thanks for your time," David said, swallowing a rush of bitter stomach acid.

A guy could get an ulcer from this much disappointment. He'd heard similar answers all weekend while he dodged the frenzy of partiers as he went from parlor to parlor all over the city. He was running out of businesses to check out.

David trudged from the tattoo parlor onto the sidewalk. Foot and vehicle traffic was sluggish this Monday evening in a San Antonio nightclub district. Neon lights and meaty, spicy scents from surrounding restaurants greeted him. The savory odors didn't stimulate so much as a drop of saliva on his taste buds.

With a long groan, he climbed into his rental car and scanned his dwindling list of unvisited tattoo parlors. Of course, in the past decade the one he needed to find might have closed its doors. His chances of locating the right parlor might be slim to none.

The phone at his belt played Pachelbel, and the screen lit with Laurel's number. David's heart jumped. Had the Montel boy been arrested? Were Laurel and Caroline in the clear?

"David here."

"Why is that security van still lurking across the street from my house?"

"Good evening to you, too. Did you just notice that little detail?"

Laurel let out an exasperated noise. "I turned in early the past few nights and didn't look outside. Tonight I did, and there sat the van. I appreciate your care for us, David. I really do, but I thought you said you would call the bodyguard off."

"I said I could. I didn't say I would. I didn't feel comfortable backing off until an arrest had been made. Has that happened?"

Several beats of silence ended in a soft sigh. "Not yet. The most likely arrest remains Caroline or me or both of us. Apparently, Grant Montel wasn't in town at the time Melissa Eldon met her demise."

"When was that?"

"My question exactly, among a number of others, but Detective Iceberg wasn't forthcoming."

David chuckled. "Iceberg. Appropriate moniker." He liked this woman's sense of humor.

"Caroline gave a statement to a female staff sergeant about the harassment and stalking, but I don't hold out large hope that much will come of it since Grant hasn't yet done anything actionable that we can prove. We were told to refer the matter to the school administration."

"Are you going to follow through with that suggestion?"

"Of course. We have an appointment with the principal next Monday."

"You don't sound very hopeful."

"I'm ninety-nine percent certain that we're opening a can of worms that won't end well for us. I may have to find a different school for Caroline. But I can't live with my conscience if I don't speak out about unacceptable behavior. So many bullies get away with their tactics for years and harass innocent victims who might have been spared if people along the way hadn't let fear stop them from making a stand."

"I'm proud of you…and Caroline. Tell her David said to hang tough."

"I'll do that. But I'm sure you're happy to be out of range of our problems. You've done a great deal. Please don't feel any further obligation to us."

"Obligation isn't my motivation."

"Then what is?"

There it was—the point blank question. What did he dare tell her? *The truth, buddy.* His conscience spoke loud and clear.

What exactly was the truth? There was such a muddle of factors. Like his natural instinct to defend the defenseless. Were his mother around, she could testify under oath about the many times he'd come home from school with a black eye or cut lip because he jumped into some fray not his own. And then there was the thorny issue of his growing attraction to Laurel as a woman and his affection for spunky Caroline. Laurel wouldn't be interested in those unquantifiable motives. There was only one reason she'd care to hear—and it was one he was overdue sharing with her.

"Melissa Eldon had a tattoo almost identical to my dead girlfriend's. They may have known each other in college ten years ago. I'm—"

"That's it? Tattoos obtained on some undergraduate whim?" Laurel's tone was incredulous.

"The design was unique. Not your run-of-the-mill flower or butterfly."

"If you think the coincidence of similar tattoos is important in finding whoever is responsible for their deaths, don't you think the police might be interested in that information?"

"Sure, but I figured their first assumption would be that I had something to do with Melissa's death, too. Before I speak up, I need to know if there's significance to the commonality—beyond some random fluke."

"Because you know you didn't kill Melissa, so if by some wild chance the tattoos connect the two murders, then you didn't kill Alicia either."

Laurel's words flowed without intonation as David sat speechless with his mouth open. She got it. Did that mean she would forgive him for not sharing this information sooner?

"You're not angry with me for keeping this to myself?"

"I'm steaming like Old Faithful ready to erupt,

Mr. Greene, but I understand your desperation. I sensed you were keeping something from us—at least it wasn't something sinister. For that small mercy I'm relieved. Good night, Mr. Greene. Call off that bodyguard. No semantic gymnastics to get off the hook this time."

The connection closed, and David rammed his head back against the headrest. She was angry all right. She'd addressed him formally twice in one string of sentences. What had he expected Laurel's reaction would be? She'd understood his thinking about the possible connection that the tattoos suggested between the two women, but then she'd called him desperate.

She was right about that. He was probably grasping for ashes in the wind. Maybe he should head home and put his feet up. Flip on the boob tube and watch sitcom reruns. Forget about Melissa and Alicia…and Laurel and Caroline, too.

No! His teeth clamped together. He couldn't abandon this long-shot lead without wringing every drop of possibility from it.

But if Laurel felt so strongly about having the watchdog stand down, he'd comply…reluctantly. He punched up the number of the business's central office and waited while it rang through. The desk clerk would notify the operative that the assignment was cancelled.

"Safety and Security Services," a pleasant female voice singsonged.

David told her what he wanted.

"Very well, sir. I'll place a call to— Just a moment, sir. The operative's emergency light just went red. I'll have to let you go so I can call the police."

THIRTEEN

This wasn't possible! Laurel's heart raced, and her breathing pumped shallow and fast.

Two minutes after requesting David remove the bodyguard, she was waiting for the security agent to burst into her home by any means necessary and save Caroline and her from whoever was downstairs.

Another thud sounded below, then a crash of breakage—one of the new lamps? An eerie, raucous cry scraped like claws down Laurel's backbone. The man with the cold! She'd been half expecting another threatening phone call since she deduced he must have her cell number. Instead, he was in their house? How? All of the locks had been changed.

Laurel's arms tightened around Caroline. The girl's slender body shuddered. The two of them were in Caroline's room behind a closed door barricaded by a wooden desk chair under the knob. The protection looked mighty flimsy.

"Mo-o-om!" The girl's familiar whimper bled forth.

"It'll be okay, sweetheart. Help is on the way."

Faint rattling drifted upstairs from the area of the front door. Must be the security guy. When she called Mack Simmons, he'd directed her to secure herself and her daughter as best she could and not to worry about letting him in. He had the equipment and skills to deal with the lock on his own, and when the alarm went off, so much the better.

The alarm blared, which meant Mack must have gained entrance. The electronic screech drowned any other noises from downstairs. Laurel drew her daughter to the bed and sat on the edge with the girl still clutched in her embrace. Both pairs of eyes stayed riveted on the door. Beneath Laurel's clinging arms, Caroline's heart fluttered like a caged bird. Laurel's wasn't much less frenzied.

A sharp report echoed through the house, and Laurel jumped with a cry. Caroline burst into tears. The gun roared again, followed by a shattering sound, faint but distinct against the backdrop of the alarm's wail. Then nothing but the alarm.

A minute passed. Then another.

Laurel scarcely dared breathe. Who had been shot down there? The intruder or their hired defender?

If the latter, then she and Caroline were on their own. Laurel eased away from her daughter and pointed to the corner of the room where Caroline's softball bat leaned against the wall. Caroline's lips trembled, but her gaze firmed as she nodded.

Laurel crossed the room and grabbed the bat. Caroline went the other direction and returned with a tennis racket. What good these weapons might be against a firearm, Laurel didn't care to contemplate.

She took up a position on one side of the barricaded door while Caroline took the other side. Laurel gazed into her daughter's eyes, so like her own in their rich shade of brown. In this moment, even though fear fixed her child's eyes wide, the pupils had darkened. Gone steady. Determined.

A strange peace wound around Laurel's heart. Yes, misunderstandings and contests of will remained ahead for the two of them. Inevitable with two such stubborn women in the household. But Caroline was going to be all right. She'd find her way through the land mines along the path to adulthood. Laurel knew that now. Provided they survived the next few minutes.

The doorknob rattled, and they raised their weapons as one.

David's cell phone played its tune, and he nearly jumped out of his skin as he paced up and down on the sidewalk in front of the last tattoo parlor he'd visited. He hadn't moved from the spot while the longest fifteen minutes of his life crawled past on hot coals. Scarcely glancing at the caller ID, he keyed to answer.

"Yes!"

"Mr. Greene?"

It was Mack. David exhaled a pent-up breath. "Are Laurel and Caroline all right?"

"Yes, sir. Shaken up and scared white, but they're troopers."

David wilted against the outside wall of the parlor. If the stucco-coated cement wasn't holding him up, he'd be on his knees literally as well as in spirit.

Mack chuckled. "If I'd been the wrong person attempting to get at them through that barricaded bedroom door, they were going to bean me with a bat and a tennis racket."

"Sounds like them." A grin began to grow on David's face. "I take it there was an intruder. Did you catch him?"

"Negative. It wasn't a human intruder. It was some kind of large bird."

"A bird?"

"Yes, and vicious, too. It attacked me. Came at me with beak and talons. I took a couple of shots at it and unfortunately managed to break the picture window in the living room. The thing flew away. Probably got in down the chimney. Critters do that sometimes when the weather gets cold. Then they don't know how to get out and go nuts."

"What kind of bird was it?"

"I don't know. Big and black. There are a few feathers lying around the living room. Maybe some bird expert can tell us— Oh, hey, the cops are here now. I'd better go."

"Have Laurel call me when she's free, would you?"

"Will do."

The connection went dead. David slid the phone into the pouch at his belt. Now a live bird was involved in this deadly mystery. He didn't for a minute think that bird got down the chimney by accident. Someone clever and vindictive was at work. A bird that could be described as having talons was a bird of prey, the kind of bird depicted by those tattoos.

David got into his car. He was going to find answers tonight. How he could force that to happen, he didn't have a clue, but that was the way it was going to be.

Forty-five minutes later, he entered a hole-in-the-wall place called simply Jake's Tattoos that looked like it had seen better days. The tools of the trade sat ready on shelves and benches, but there were no customers lying on tables or reclining in chairs. Scents of ink and blood pervaded the air the same as they had in the other parlors David had visited. He was almost getting used to the odor.

"What can I do for you, man?" A youth with scruffy shoulder-length hair and a wisp of a goatee rose from behind the counter wearing a lopsided smile. "We've got some great specials going."

"I'm tracking down the origins of a particular design." David presented the photo on his phone and braced himself for another blank stare. The kid didn't look old enough to be in college himself, much less old enough to have been in the tattoo business a decade ago.

The young man frowned at the photo, started to shake his head then peered more closely. "Do you mind?" He reached for the phone.

David released it to him. The kid flicked on a gooseneck lamp and studied the picture while he stroked his goatee.

"Can't tell for sure," he said at last, "cuz the photo's not the best. Looks like there were white flecks in the air between the lens and the subject. Ashes?"

"Snow. What are you thinking but not saying?" Throttling the information from this young man could be a viable option at the moment. David's hands fisted, and the tips of his fingernails bit into his palms.

The kid flicked the photo to zoom in on the image and let out a hum. "Looks like my grandfather's work. Nobody—but nobody—did a talon like Grandpa Jake."

"The Jake from the name above the door."

"That's him. People used to come from around the world for his work if they needed something with a bird or a dragon in it. He was a true artist."

David's heart hit his toes. "Was?"

"Retired now. Couldn't do a tat if his life depended on it. Arthritis in his joints." The kid's mouth drooped.

David inhaled, then exhaled a cleansing breath of air. "Would it be possible to talk to your grandfather?"

"Prob'ly." The young man smiled. "He lives in the apartment upstairs."

Within twenty minutes, David had more answers than he'd wanted. He staggered out to his car and leaned on the hood. A fist—no, talons—clutched his heart.

Maybe he was jumping to conclusions. Maybe— forget it! No maybe. The facts fit too neatly to call his thoughts a flight of fancy. His gut chewed on itself.

Pachelbel began to play. David swiped the phone from his belt and narrowed his eyes at the caller ID.

"Hello, Laurel." Did his voice sound as cold as he felt? "I wish I could say it's good to hear from you."

"David? What's going on? Are you all right?"

Less than a half hour ago, that would have been his question for her. Now he had a different one. "Where did you attend college?"

"I got my master's degree right here in Denver from—"

"No. You mentioned you met your ex-husband when you were a freshman in college. Where was that?" As if he didn't know the answer.

"San Antonio. I—"

"That's what I thought. I'm flying back to Denver tonight. I'll be on your doorstep first thing in the morning."

"We're at Janice's again until that picture window can be replaced."

"Of course. Be prepared to answer more questions. Lots more."

"David, you're scaring me."

"You can't be half as scared as I am."

FOURTEEN

"What has gotten into you, David?" Crossing her arms, Laurel stared into David's storm-cloud eyes.

They glared at each other across the length of Janice's family room.

"Do the words Jeweled Talon Society mean anything to you?"

"Should they? Get to the point, will you? My life has been terrorized enough. I don't need any more suspense."

"Five women—" David raised his left hand with the digits spread apart "—freshmen at the same college, each one an outstanding beauty, made a pact to wed only wealthy men. In fact, it was a contest to see who could snare the wealthiest husband. They sealed the pact by each getting the tattoo of a raven's talons gripping a jewel—every jewel as unique and beautiful as they were. They wore their tattoos right here." He lifted his left hand to cover a spot below the breastbone but above the heart. "Starting to ring a bell?"

The bitter twist of his lips jabbed Laurel's heart like a knife. "No bells. No whistles. Not even a gong. Where did you discover this information, and what does a shameful pact have to do with my situation?"

A realization zapped through Laurel's brain and she gasped, covering her mouth with her fingers.

Heat flared in David's gaze. "Suddenly remembering?"

"You mean Alicia and Melissa had these tattoos? They were part of this foolishness? Do you think something to do with this Raven Jewel Society got them killed?"

David expelled a burst of air. "Jeweled Talon Society—as if you didn't know. Laurel, it's time for the truth. You admitted to me you were a freshman at the University of Texas in San Antonio."

"No, David, I said I started college in San Antonio, but you never let me finish my sentence to tell you which school. I was a freshman at Northwest Vista College."

If she'd brained him with that bat she held in her hands last night, he couldn't look more stunned. Served him right for leaping to conclusions. She was on a roll and not about to back off.

Laurel marched up to him and poked a finger into his breastbone. "I never finished that first year of college because a narcissistic shark who thought his money could buy me body, soul and spirit conned my starry-eyed younger self into believing he was my knight in shining armor. I never got to go back to school until after the divorce, and I did it on my own—with God's grace, and not a dime of his filthy lucre."

"But—"

She jabbed his breastbone again. "You think I'm wearing a tattoo under this sweater?" She yanked the neck down to expose her collarbone. "Never had a tat. Never plan to get one. Satisfied?"

David's gaze rolled upward, then down and captured hers. "Thank You, Jesus!"

Joy burst across his face, but then she couldn't see his expression because her nose was mashed up against his shoulder. Powerful arms wrapped her close. Her body ached to relax into the embrace, but she stood stiff. Stunned and energized at the same time. Did she even know how to let a man hold her?

"I was petrified!" His breath ruffled the hair by her ear. "Thinking you might be one of the Talons hurt so bad I thought it might kill me. I'm so glad. So thankful."

Laurel wriggled against him, and he released her. She stepped back, wary gaze fixed on him. "I'm glad you're glad, but I'm confused. And I'm still angry that you thought for one moment that I could be a part of this…this…whatever it is."

David backpedaled to one of the easy chairs and plopped into it. "Have a seat, and I'll tell you what I found out about the tattoos." He ran his fingers through his hair, leaving the thick waves in pleasing disarray. "Apparently someone else also knows the significance of these tats, and he must have come to the same conclusion about your involvement as I did. A big, black bird of prey was let loose in your house last night. It's not much of a leap of logic to think the creature was a raven."

The awful sense of David's statements struck Laurel, and she sank into the chair opposite his. "I can see how easily carrying out a pact such as you're describing could make bitter enemies. If someone has it in for these Talon women, that person might be responsible for the deaths of Alicia Gonzales and Melissa Eldon."

"Bingo." David jerked a nod. "Last night I located the tattoo artist who painted all five of the co-eds. He remembers the incident vividly. These five raving beauties descended on his shop demanding identical tats, except for the type of jewel held in each set of talons. From chatter between the ladies while he was doing the work, he pieced together the gist of this pact and the arrogant name they called their little clique. He told me that if he hadn't needed the cash, he would have booted their shapely bottoms out onto the street."

Laurel leaned forward. "Why would anyone think I was a part of this? Why did *you?*"

"Who you married—an obscenely wealthy man. Where you started school—the city anyway. And what you look like."

"What I look like?"

"The participants were one Nordic Amazon with blue eyes—"

"Melissa." Laurel nodded.

"One Hispanic bombshell with ebony hair and eyes—"

"Alicia."

"A willowy redhead with green eyes, a statuesque brunette with amber eyes and a petite heart-stealer with honey blond hair and enormous brown eyes."

"Me?" Laurel poked a thumb at herself. "I've never thought of myself as a heart-stealer." She wrinkled her nose.

"Trust me, you are."

She warmed beneath David's grin and looked away, gnawing her lower lip. "Steven's second wife—the woman he replaced me with—looked enough like me to be my sister. And she had a tattoo right where you described. I met her once and caught a glimpse of ink. Just not enough to make out the design."

David breathed out a low whistle. "Somebody got his wires crossed between the two of you. The golden blonde and the one with coal black hair are already dead. The honey blonde—who our killer thinks is you—is under attack. I wonder where the brunette and redhead are, or if they're dead, too."

"What did you say?"

"I wonder if they're dead—"

"No, you listed the hair colors. Golden blonde, black, honey blonde, brunette and redhead. I had five china figurines with exactly those shades of hair. And the eye colors matched your descriptions of these women."

David nodded. "I remember picking up the pieces of those figurines, but I didn't notice what all the hair and eye colors were. Caroline told me you got those figurines as a gift from—"

"Janice!" Laurel finished David's sentence, then hit her knees on the carpet and grabbed his hands. "Janice is a redhead. She colors her hair chestnut, because she says the red is too vivid for some of her stuffy, high-end clients. And she's got a scar right here." She patted beneath her collar bone. "It's faint, but it shows up in the summer when she tans in her bathing suit. It's the kind of scar you'd get from having a tattoo removed."

David raised an eyebrow. "Was Kurt one of those humble millionaires who preferred to live in a middle-class neighborhood?"

"Hardly." Laurel laughed. "Kurt was a regular working guy, not even that good-looking, but he and Janice loved each other deeply. Kurt wasn't her first husband, though. She had a nightmare of a marriage to a rich, older man who cheated on her constantly and then divorced her without a dime or a backward look."

Laurel rocked back on her heels. A shiver coursed through her, and she let out a moan. "I can't believe this. My best friend is a Talon!"

David dropped to his knees in front of her and

gripped her upper arms. "Worse. Could she be the one eliminating the other Talons?"

"No!" Laurel shook her head and broke free of him. "She knows I'm not a Talon."

"If she's still in possession of her sanity. Who knows what happens in people's minds when they go homicidal."

"I don't buy it, David." Laurel rose. "She was out of the country when Alicia was murdered."

He snorted. "Wonderful alibi, don't you think? Isn't it odd she hasn't mentioned knowing Melissa Eldon?"

"It's not that odd if she wanted her past to remain in the past. Why would she think Melissa's death would have any connection to some co-ed foolishness from ten years ago?"

"Merely stating that she knew the woman in college would hardly be incriminating, but she didn't say a word."

Laurel frowned. Was she being stubborn? Refusing to see the truth? But she owed Janice so much. The woman had been there for her and Caroline through every hard knock of life. They'd told each other secrets about themselves no one else knew— except for this glaring omission. The Talon business was pretty huge to leave out.

"Yes, I have doubts," she said. "But I'm not ready to condemn her. In fact, she could be in danger if someone really is targeting the Talons."

"Where is she? And where's Caroline?"

"Oh, no!" Laurel's pulse stalled.

"What?"

"I knew you were headed our way with a bone to pick, and I didn't want her or Caroline to be here. When Janice suggested we go out for breakfast this morning, I told the two of them to go on without me. Didn't even mention you were coming. Janice said she was going to take Caroline with her to a house showing after they ate."

Laurel looked at her watch. "They've been gone nearly three hours. They should be back by now."

She grabbed her cell phone from a side table. The call rang until it went to voice mail. Laurel's stomach turned at Janice's perky message. Could this woman she thought she knew actually be a calculating manipulator? That wasn't the Janice Laurel knew...or thought she knew. If Janice's best friend act had been just that—an act—had Laurel sent her daughter off to breakfast with a killer?

"Let's check Janice's office," she said, laying her phone on the small table. "Maybe we can find out something that will tell us where they went for the house showing."

"Lead the way."

They skirted the kitchen, went up the hall and then turned a corner through French doors into a spacious office. All the tools of a business were there—fax machine, copier, printer and a large desk that served as home to a landline, a computer and numerous file folders, forms and assorted glossy fliers.

"Does she have an appointment calendar?" David asked.

"It would be on her computer as well as the PDA she carries with her everywhere."

David wiggled the mouse, and the computer screen lit up. "Do you know her password?"

"No." Laurel flapped her arms against her sides.

"Let's start looking. People sometimes keep their passwords handy under their phone or the mouse pad or somewhere like that." He lifted the pad up and shook his head.

Faint music from the family room reached Laurel's ears. "My phone! Maybe it's her."

"Maybe. You go check, and I'll keep looking."

Tight knot in her middle, Laurel scurried up the hallway. *Please let it be Janice. I need to know that Caroline is okay.* But even as she prayed, her heart throbbed like a mashed thumb. What could she say to this friend who might more aptly be named Judas than Janice?

She picked up the phone. The caller wasn't who she'd hoped. The ID window said Unknown Number. Laurel's pulse became staccato hoof beats in her ears.

"Hello?" The greeting emerged a croak.

"If you want your daughter to live to see another day, leave the house now and meet me in the south parking lot of the Cherry Creek Shopping Center."

The deep rasp sounded male, but a woman could mimic such a tone, or even use an electronic device to create the effect.

"Tell no one," the voice went on. "Speak to no one. Leave our phone connection open so I can hear everything happening around you, and so you cannot place any calls or send any texts. You have ten minutes to arrive. Eleven minutes will be too late for pretty Caroline."

"Ten minutes isn't much time."

"Then you'd best hurry."

"Janice?"

The caller chuckled. "Your daughter is your only concern."

Had this maniac already done something to Janice? A soundless scream echoed through Laurel's brain. But he was right, Caroline must come first.

"I—I'm grabbing my jacket now." She scurried to the entryway by the kitchen.

Small sounds of a search issued from up the hallway. Laurel dared not attempt to get David's attention. He was too likely to speak, ask questions, which would alert this psycho that she'd communicated with someone.

David! If only you could hear my heart's cry for help! God, are You there?

If Janice kept a written reminder of her password anywhere on her desk, David was at a loss to find it. He picked up a sheaf of papers, but several fell from his grip and fluttered to the floor. As he bent to pick them up, a name leaped out at him from the top sheet.

Gilbert Montel.

David scanned the document. It was a representation agreement for Janice to act as seller's agent. Gil was selling his house? The form was dated a couple of weeks ago, around the time the millionaire became engaged to Melissa Eldon. Did Melissa want them to move out of the house where Gil had lived with his first wife? Not an uncommon scenario.

Is that how Janice became aware that one of her sister Talons was about to score large? Did she eliminate Melissa because she had set her sights on Gil for herself?

Knowing what he now did about the Jeweled Talon Society, Laurel's friend had motive and opportunity, but Laurel might be glad to know he wasn't sold on her guilt. After all, if the woman were still on the prowl for rich prey, why had she remained single for so long?

But if Janice was innocent, why had she never told Laurel she was seller's agent to the murdered woman's fiancé? That detail seemed rather pertinent under the circumstances. When they caught up with Janice, she had some tall explaining to do. If an innocent explanation was even possible.

David set the paper on the Realtor's desk and took out his cell phone. Whether Laurel liked it or not, he needed to communicate this new evidence to Detective Berg. All of it. And let the investigation take its course. At minimum, Laurel and Caroline should find themselves in the clear. He hardly dared hope he might be exonerated also.

Thankfully, he caught the detective at his desk. Quickly and concisely, David presented his discoveries. Berg remained silent until David had finished, then asked a few clarifying questions.

At last, a long sigh carried over the connection. "I'd like to arrest you for withholding information in a murder investigation, but I'm not sure the charge would stick. You pursued a long shot, and it paid off. Be content and back off. Let us do our job."

"I understand, sir. Laurel and I are particularly concerned about the whereabouts of her friend Janice and her daughter, Caroline. Laurel got a phone call a few minutes ago. It could have been her friend, but she hasn't come back with that information."

"Go see. I'll stay on the line."

David walked to the family room, but found it empty. Eerie silence draped the house. Calling Laurel's name, he hurried to the front room. A window offered a view of Laurel's house next door, and a car with her at the wheel was careening backward out of the driveway.

"Something about that phone call just sent Laurel to her car without saying a word to me," he told Berg. "I'm going to follow."

"What did I tell you about letting us do our job?"

"You aren't here. I am. I'll keep you informed until someone from the P.D. can pick up the trail."

"You do that."

The detective's bark barely registered as David keyed off his phone, flung on his jacket and sprinted to his rental car. *Please, God, don't let me lose her.* He burned rubber in a U-turn, but Laurel's vehicle had disappeared from view. David gunned the V-8 engine, and the vehicle leaped forward. Good thing he'd indulged his penchant for powerful cars at the airport rental agency.

Up several blocks, he spotted her vehicle fading in the distance on a side road. Apparently, she was headed toward the nearest interstate on-ramp. His vehicle ate up the distance between him and her economy rental. If she spotted him, would she try to lose him? He couldn't worry about that. Just stay on her tail.

He drew up several car lengths behind her. Her brake lights winked at him in a pair of short bursts—a deliberate move—and he smiled. She wasn't trying to lose him. He could only conclude she needed help. Why hadn't she told him before she left?

He keyed in her phone number, but the call went straight to voice mail. Either she'd been ordered to turn off her phone, or the connection was still live with someone who didn't want her communicating with anyone else. This creep was beyond clever. The strongest button anyone could push with Laurel was something to do with Caroline.

Redness edged David's vision. That kid was a hot button with him, too. If he got to this guy before the cops—no, he couldn't let fury cloud his mind. He clamped down on his emotions.

Danger to Janice would be a close second with Laurel—unless, of course, Janice was the culprit all along.

They hit the interstate ramp at a ridiculous rate of speed. David called Detective Berg and gave him their location. "Can you trace Laurel by her cell GPS?"

"Only if she's using the phone."

"Give it a shot." He rattled off the number that had stuck in his head as firmly as the beautiful woman with whom it was associated.

"We're on it. Stay on the line with me from now on. I'm in my vehicle en route to intercept."

Berg's voice grew distant as he issued instructions to someone in the car with him. Probably his partner. A radio bleeped, and the partner's voice barked indistinct orders into it.

"We're exiting toward Cherry Creek Shopping Center," he told the detective.

"If she's meeting someone, hang back. Don't let yourself be seen."

"Only if Laurel's not in imminent danger."

A curse answered that stipulation. "We're less than two minutes behind you."

David firmed his jaw. A lot could happen in that amount of time.

Laurel's car turned in to a mall entrance. David signaled to turn in after her, but another vehicle surged in front of him, exiting the lot. He slammed on the brakes, and the teenage boy behind the wheel of the other car made a rude gesture as he sped away. David whisked into the lot, gaze roaming for Laurel's car and coming up blank. Just that fast, he'd lost her.

Pulse pounding, he relayed to the detective what had happened and received reassurances of their imminent arrival.

"Sit tight," Berg added. "Her phone is live, and we've got her on GPS."

Eternal seconds later, the unmarked police vehicle glided past David's car. He followed at a discrete distance around the perimeter of the parking lot to the other side of the mall. His heart leaped. There was Laurel's vehicle sitting alone at the farthest edge of the lot near a busy street. The driver's door hung wide open.

David slammed on the brakes and made a rocking park, then leaped out and raced toward Laurel's car on the tails of the pair of detectives. They'd have to arrest him to stop him from looking. Over their shoulders, he peered into Laurel's vehicle. The car was empty except for her cell phone lying on the passenger seat.

He stared wildly around, but any of dozens of

vehicles in motion on the street or in the parking lot could contain a kidnap victim. His shoulders slumped. When she needed him the most, he'd failed the woman who had come to mean more to him than his next heartbeat.

Why did he realize how precious she was to him when he might never get the chance to tell her?

FIFTEEN

Where...am...I?

The question floated through Laurel's brain. Ephemeral. Wispy. As if her mind were detached from the earth.

A steady hum filled her ears, and a gentle vibration shook her body where she lay curled on her side. If only she could open her eyes. Ah, yes. They *were* open. Darkness filled them. Her nose was filled with something else—an oily, metallic scent. She willed her arms to move, to stretch out and explore her surroundings, but they refused to respond.

She'd been kidnapped!

Awareness shot adrenaline to her extremities, and she stiffened.

David! He'd been following her. What a good man. She no longer possessed a single doubt of his innocence. The monster who had taken her had also killed Alicia. If only David were here to hold her. She would snuggle close. Safe. But she didn't know what had become of him. Was he all right?

She'd parked her car as directed next to a black sedan. A thickset man wearing dark clothing and a ski mask got out, soft-footed to her door, opened it and reached in. She didn't even have time to scream before a prick at the back of her neck put the lights out.

The lights were still out, but she was no longer unconscious. Was she in the car's trunk? A moan escaped her lips, and she managed to spread the fingers of one of her hands against what felt like nubby fabric. Trunk carpet.

If so, there ought to be a fluorescent latch somewhere in here that would release the trunk cover. Nothing fluorescent gleamed in her environment. Her captor could have removed it and disabled the latch. That move made sense if he planned to use his trunk as a prison.

Thankfully, she wasn't bound or gagged. Laurel swallowed against a desert-dry throat. If she regained enough command of her body, she might be able to do what she'd read about in one of those women's magazines. She could punch out one of the taillights, reach through and wave for help at oncoming traffic.

Yes, that's what she'd do. Groans echoing in the small space, she rolled onto her back.

A soft hiss sounded, then a strange sweetish odor clogged her nostrils…and then nothing.

Nearly two hours later, David sat slumped in his car in the mall parking lot. He'd undergone extensive grilling as he gave his statement to the detectives. Berg had been particularly interested in every detail about the Jeweled Talon Society. While they talked, evidence technicians showed up and processed the scene before towing away Laurel's rental car for microscopic examination—the second vehicle she'd lost to that fate in recent history.

Now the detective sat in his unmarked sedan a few feet away, talking on the phone. David started his car. Maybe that would get the hint across that he'd like clearance to leave. Besides, the afternoon sun that beat on the roof of his dark blue rental only managed to warm the interior marginally against a bitter chill that had moved into the Denver area overnight.

Berg got out of his sedan and sauntered over. David rolled down the window, and the detective leaned inside. A noticeable thaw was visible in the gaze that lit on David.

"Still no sign of Janice Swenson or Caroline Adams," Berg said. "The crew that scoured Mrs. Swenson's house for clues to her whereabouts turned up a notation in her office that placed her at a vacant house for a showing this morning. A black-and-white dropped by and found evidence of a scuffle."

"Evidence? You mean like blood?" David's marrow chilled.

"Some. Not enough to be sure anything life threatening occurred."

"But you can't rule it out."

"Unfortunately not. The crew at Mrs. Swenson's turned up something else of interest."

David narrowed his eyes. "What might that be?"

"Potassium cyanide. The kind used by entomologists in killing jars."

"Janice's late husband collected and displayed butterflies. What's so… You mean Melissa Eldon died of cyanide poisoning?"

Berg backed away and rose to his full height, wearing a Cheshire cat grin. "You hole up somewhere now and let us do our job. Here's my card in case you think of anything else we should know."

David took the rectangle of card stock, and watched the detective join his partner in their car. Gnawing the inside of his cheek, David stared after the departing vehicle.

So suspicion had traveled from Laurel and Caroline to Janice. Or maybe now the cops were thinking the three of them were in cahoots on the death of Melissa Eldon. Then how did they explain Laurel's apparent kidnapping, as well as the disappearance of Caroline and Janice amidst "signs of a scuffle?" Maybe they figured this whole scenario was a scheme to divert suspicion. Someone's labyrinthine mind needed rerouting. But how could he help that happen?

Think, man, think!

His gaze fell to the sheet of paper he'd clutched

in his fist as he ran out to the car. It gleamed at him from the passenger seat in black and white. Maybe all roads converged upon the address written on the Realtor's representation agreement.

Gil Montel's sister was murdered by her groom, Lawrence Taylor, while on their honeymoon. Lawrence, a wealthy man with many resources at his disposal, had escaped and disappeared. It wasn't a large leap of the imagination to think that this man might kill other women. How he'd crossed paths with the Jeweled Talon Society remained a mystery…unless Paula was a Talon.

Heart thumping, David conjured up a mental image of the shrine Gil had constructed to his sister. Paula had been a stunning, amber-eyed brunette, the same as one of the Talons they hadn't accounted for. But that wasn't the only detail his brain was struggling to recall. Hadn't there been some sort of clue to an organization with which she'd been connected? Yes! A pendant bearing the initials UTSA—University of Texas at San Antonio. Of course!

Breath hissed between David's teeth. Was Paula dead because through her callous pact she'd triggered the rage of an arrogant man who discovered he'd been suckered by the oldest game in the book? Maybe Gil had answers he didn't know he knew. David just had to ask the right questions.

He started the car and peeled out of the parking

lot. A couple of miles down the road, his cell phone began to play. The ID said Unknown Caller. Heat spiked down David's spine as he tapped to answer.

"Hello, you pathetic excuse for a human being. Where are the women? Where's Caroline?"

The person at the other end tsked. "If you wish to keep this dialogue open, try a little respect," a harsh voice rasped. "Name-calling where you know nothing is inappropriate."

"I know one thing." David schooled his tone to an intense whisper.

"Good for you. What is that?"

"It's going to take more than a voice-altering device to hide your identity."

"You know who I am then?"

"You've killed before."

"Brilliant deduction! I'm starting to enjoy this conversation. When? Before who?"

"Before Melissa. Before Alicia. Four years ago." The slightest sound of indrawn breath betrayed surprise from the mocker at the other end of the connection. Dark satisfaction expanded in David's chest. "And you got away with it. Until now. Because you couldn't stop!"

"*You're* going to stop me?"

"Me. The police. Someone. Soon."

"Before or after fair Caroline either asphyxiates or freezes to death?"

Words stalled on David's lips.

"Now that I have your attention, let the game begin."

"Game?" The question spat between David's teeth.

"A simple round of geocaching. Your coordinates are being texted to you." Accordingly, David's cell phone pinged. "It will be unnecessary for us to speak again." A laugh began but was abruptly cut off into blank air.

Thumb quivering, David brought up the text message.

Caroline in danger? Freezing? Gasping for air?

Blanking his mind of how that awesome kid could be suffering, he entered the coordinates into his GPS app. The impersonal female voice instructed him to reverse his course. Following her directives, he drove at the maximum speed he dared without getting stopped by a traffic cop. Minutes counted. Maybe even seconds.

In the mall parking lot, Detective Berg had given David his direct line number. David punched it in and waited. The call went to voice mail. Suppressing a foul word, he left a terse request for Berg to call him back as soon as possible because he might have a lead on Caroline's whereabouts.

On the other hand, David was realistic enough about the twisted nature of this murderer to realize the whole geocaching exercise could be nothing more than a sadistic trick. But he couldn't risk re-

fusing to play along. Not if there was a chance that
Caroline needed him.

And what of Laurel? Without any direct clues to
her whereabouts, he had no choice but to entrust
her to the resources of the police.

As the navigation voice commanded him to turn
onto Federal Boulevard, a familiar structure came
into view. Sports Authority Field. He'd attended a
Broncos-Cowboys football game here a couple of
years back. The stadium loomed mammoth and silent.

He turned obediently onto Twentieth Avenue and
then into VIP parking lot G. At the far end of the lot
sat a black sedan. The coordinates led him straight
to it. David parked a little way back, and got out,
leaving his car idling.

He approached the other vehicle on cautious feet,
gaze darting in every direction. A bomb planted in
the abandoned vehicle wasn't out of the question, but
what choice did he have other than to investigate?
Every hair on his body stood at high alert. Biting
wind swooped and howled around him. He could
almost hear an echo of the killer's cruel laughter.

No, that wasn't laughter. It was weeping. Hoarse
sobs. Gasping breath. David's footsteps quickened.
The heartrending sounds were coming from the
trunk of the car.

"I'm here!" he cried. "David's here."

A weak wail answered him before it cut off into
a choke.

David rushed to the driver's-side door, but the vehicle was locked. "Sick monster!" He raced back to his car, opened the trunk and retrieved the tire iron.

This might be a football stadium, but today the only score that mattered relied upon a baseball swing. Standing by the driver's side window, he drew back with the tire iron, then let fly. Glass shattered everywhere, stinging like little bees attacking his face. David ignored the pain as he plunged his hand inside and held the button to release the trunk latch. A satisfying pop sounded.

He ran to the rear of the vehicle and flung open the trunk. Caroline lay inside, not bound and gagged but barely moving. Tiny whimpers dribbled between swollen, blue lips. Her whole face and neck were puffed to twice their normal size. She wore no jacket, only her sweater and jeans, but the cold wouldn't have caused the swelling. Nor would lack of oxygen.

Allergic reaction? Poison?

David scooped the girl up, clutched her close to his chest and ran for his vehicle. He scooted into the backseat where there was warmth, but also room to strip off his jacket and wrap it around her. She was semiconscious, each inhalation a truncated hiccup.

He swiped his phone from his belt and punched in 9-1-1. His terse description of the situation and their location brought a promise that help was on the way.

David dropped his phone and gathered Caroline in his arms, soul clamoring with silent prayers.

Cradling and rocking her, he crooned reassurances even as his heart threatened to shatter into a billion pieces.

Sure, help was on the way…but would it arrive in time?

Intense shivering rattled Laurel to awareness. Chill invaded her body from every angle, especially beneath her where she lay prone on a frozen surface. Pebble-size lumps bit into her back. What was that clacking sound? Oh, it was her teeth chattering. Not only *her* teeth, someone else's. She wasn't alone in this pitch blackness smelling of dirt and must.

Where was she? Where were *they?* Who was the other person?

"W-who's there?" Her voice quavered forth.

A groan answered her.

Laurel stretched her arms out to her sides, disturbing small stones and what felt like loose soil. She raised her arms, and her hands and wrists knocked against what sounded and felt like wood. The ceiling of this enclosed space was only a couple of feet above her. Good thing she hadn't tried to sit up. She would have hit her head.

Whatever drug she'd been given had worn off. She was stiff with cold but she could move.

"Laurel?"

The nearby whisper contained barely enough strength to reach Laurel's ears. She knew that voice.

"Janice?"

A sniffle answered. "I'm so cold!" The voice had strengthened, but only a little.

"Are you injured?"

"Yes. Where's Caroline?"

"Isn't she here...wherever here is?"

"I...don't think s—" Another groan cut off the sentence.

A surge of adrenaline shot tingles to Laurel's rapidly numbing extremities. They had to get out of this frigid prison and find Caroline.

"Where are you hurt?"

"Ribs. Face. Stomach. I fought...protect Caroline...but self-defense training doesn't help much... when your attacker uses a drug."

"Who was he?"

"Don't know. He wore a knitted ski mask. Ambushed us at the house where we'd gone for the showing."

"Sounds like the same man who got me. Can you move?"

"Not sure. Doesn't matter. If you can find a way, get out of here. Leave me. Rescue Caroline."

Laurel rolled onto her side, and pain sparkled up and down her back and bottom as blood flowed faster beneath iced skin.

An extended hand discovered smooth cashmere and beneath it an arm. "Janice?"

"Yes."

"You're not wearing your coat."

"Tell me about it." An attempt at a laugh ended in a moan.

Laurel patted herself. Her jacket had been removed, too. The slimeball had stashed them out of sight, yet exposed the pair of them to the cold. From all appearances, he intended them to freeze to death. Were they in the crawl space under a building? If so, there must be a trapdoor through which their captor had lowered them into the area.

"Hang tough. I'm going to explore."

Bile rose in Laurel's throat. Spider webs numbered among her least favorite things, and in a space like this they were likely to abound. At least at these temperatures, the webs' owners wouldn't be alive and apt to crawl down her arms.

Laurel got to work. Using Janice as her focal point, she worked her way in various directions, rapping and pressing against the wood above. She discovered no give in the planks. And she had yet to find any side slats where she might be able to kick free. Not that her nearly numb feet would be much good for that endeavor.

Wait! What was that? The suspicion of warm air touched her cheeks. She moved toward the sensation. Yes, a measure of heat radiated through the floorboards in this one spot. Was she underneath a furnace or a fireplace? No matter. She and Janice needed to huddle together here in order to survive past the next hour.

Hypothermia was setting in. Shivering was giving way to lethargy and clumsy movements. Janice was probably worse off, considering her injuries. Laurel had to maintain consciousness long enough to get them both settled beneath this window of warmth.

"Janice?"

No answer. Heart in her throat, Laurel felt her way in the direction she thought Janice had been. Finally—thankfully—her fingers connected with Janice's sweater. She tugged. The arm moved limply. Grasping her friend's wrist, Laurel felt for a pulse. It was there, but weak and sluggish.

Laurel took a good grip on Janice's arm and began to pull. With her height and build, Janice probably outweighed Laurel by twenty pounds. That factor, along with Laurel's growing weakness, slowed progress to inches at a time, rather than feet. But at last, they both lay beneath the steady radiation of warmth—though not outright heat—from above. Laurel wrapped her body around her friend and pulled her close.

Shortly, Janice moaned and stirred. "Did you… get us out? I told you…leave me."

"I haven't found a way to escape. Just a warmer spot." This wasn't the time or the place Laurel wanted to confront the woman she'd regarded for years as her best friend, but there might never be another opportunity. "Janice, I have to know something. Are you a member of the Jeweled Talon Society?"

The body she clutched stiffened and ceased to breathe. Then Janice began to sob.

Praying urgently as he clenched and unclenched his fists, David watched the ambulance race away from Sports Authority Field. The EMTs had responded with every bit of the speed and professionalism he could have wished, yet Caroline's life still hung in the balance. The looks on their faces had told him that much, as well as terse phrases like "emergency tracheotomy" and ominous words like *epinephrine* and *stat*.

The best thing he could do for Caroline right now was find her mother—alive! David piled into his car. Time to pursue the hunch he'd been following when evil called him on the phone. That evil had to be stopped.

Nearly twenty minutes later, David punched the call button outside Gil's estate. The very proper housekeeper answered.

"David Greene here. It's vital that I speak with Mr. Montel immediately."

"I'm sorry. Mr. Montel is busy in his office and has requested no visitors."

"Please tell him that this is a matter of life and death, and it concerns the murder of his sister, Paula."

Silence reigned for long minutes. Had she gone to carry out his request?

"I'm sorry." The woman's voice blared through

the speaker. "But Mr. Montel will not see you, Mr. Greene."

David's gut churned. What was Gil hiding? Was he really there, or was his housekeeper covering for him? Not much of an alibi if Gil were involved in something illegal—like murdering women. David frowned. Had he come to the wrong conclusion about the vicious groom being the culprit? Maybe that shrine to Paula was a sick mind's penance.

Politeness had run its course. David backed the rental car away from the gate, revved the giant motor and then unleashed the vehicle. The gate was no match for raw horsepower. Screeching, the metal doors gave way. David roared up the driveway. When he reached the house, he mashed on the brakes, threw the car in Park and charged up the steps.

The front door wasn't locked—yet. The housekeeper was scurrying toward it as David burst inside. The plump woman shrieked and ran the other direction, yelping about calling the police. He needed to work fast and be gone, or he'd be in lockup too quickly to help Laurel.

David strode up the hallway and flung wide the double doors of Gil's study. Half expecting to find the room empty, he halted just over the threshold, mouth agape.

Gil Montel sat behind his desk, snifter in hand, nearly empty brandy decanter at his elbow. Bleary eyes regarded David.

"Whatsh the meaning of thish intrusion?" The man wobbled to his feet.

"Did your sister have a tattoo below her left collar bone?"

Gil's eyes narrowed. "How did you know?"

"Was it a raven's talons gripping a jewel?"

"Shum bird'sh claw." Gil waved a dismissive hand.

"Would you be surprised to know that the man who killed your sister also killed your fiancée, Melissa, and my girlfriend, Alicia? That tattoo links all three of them, plus two more."

Gil's lips parted, but his only response was a blank stare.

"These women were part of a pact to seduce wealthy men with their beauty," David said. "Now this vengeful man has kidnapped a child, Caroline Adams, and left her dying of an allergic reaction to some kind of chemical he dosed her with. Plus, he's taken another woman, as well as Caroline's mother—a fine person whose only crime is to physically resemble someone who was a part of this ungodly sorority."

"What dosh thish have to do with me?"

"I think the person responsible is your former brother-in-law. Where would Lawrence take those women?" David strode across the room and put his face in Gil's. "Think! Was there any place in the area that he and Paula liked to go? Someplace secluded?"

The other man's pudgy cheeks sank into his jaw, and he collapsed onto his chair with a sob. David gazed down at Gil Montel's balding head and shaking shoulders. If he could knock the slightest information out of this pitiful specimen, he wouldn't hesitate, but he was fighting a losing battle.

"Thanks for nothing."

David strode from the room and up the hallway. Any minute he could expect to hear sirens approaching, and now he had no more leads to follow. He'd failed Laurel again.

"David Greene!"

The bark of his name brought David to a halt. Grant hurried toward him, eyes blazing, something crumpled in his fist. David braced himself. Was he about to be assaulted by a teenager?

The young man stopped in front of him, chest heaving. "I overheard. Caroline's…dead?"

"She was fighting for her life when the ambulance took her away."

"Here!" Grant extended his hand and opened his fist. A crumpled newspaper article lay in his palm. "Now you should go. I told the houscekeeper not to call the cops, but she might not listen to me."

David gingerly accepted the segment of yellowed newsprint. Grant whirled on his heel and ran away. The bowels of the house swallowed his lanky figure.

Paper in hand, David hurried to his car and drove out the gate. Though he heard no sirens, he lost himself deep in the residential neighborhood, then pulled over to the curb and opened the wadded-up newsprint.

Blood congealed in his veins. No need to read the article. The photograph and the caption beneath it told the story. David knew where he needed to look.

If he wasn't already too late.

SIXTEEN

"I never wanted you to know," Janice rasped. "I'm so ashamed. We were a capricious gaggle of fools—all thinking we had good reason to despise men, wealthy ones in particular. We convinced ourselves that we were on a holy mission to use our God-given assets—our looks—to punish them. We only punished ourselves."

Laurel's heart beat erratically against her ribs. How could she ever look at Janice with the same trust and affection again? Did she want to hear the rest of this bizarre story? But how could she not, considering what was at stake?

"Go on," she said. "I have to know who might have stashed us here—who might yet have Caroline, if he hasn't already—" Laurel choked on finishing the awful sentence.

"I don't expect you to forgive me." A shuddering breath heaved from the woman Laurel held close but wanted to shove away. "We had no idea what terrible events we were setting in motion. Many lives have been torn apart. Most of us are dead."

"Other than you and Melissa Eldon, who was part of this pact?"

"I didn't know Melissa with the last name of Eldon. She must have had a marriage in between our college days and when she landed in Denver as a schoolteacher—which, by the way, was a totally out-of-character occupation for her. She thought people should be born adults and skip the messiness and dependency of childhood. I think her childhood must have been horrible, but I never knew the details."

"Didn't you recognize her face on the news broadcasts?"

"You know me and the news. Can't even stand to have a television in the house."

"An odd phobia that you've glossed over as a personal idiosyncrasy. There's got to be a deeper story."

"Another time. If we live, and you still want to talk to me."

Laurel had no answer for that. "Who else was a Talon?"

"Fernanda Gonzales—"

"Fernanda? David's girlfriend's name was Alicia."

"Really! I'm not surprised Fern changed her name. She hated the one her parents had given her almost as much as she hated *them*."

"So after you got back from your tour of Europe, if anyone mentioned the notorious Alicia Gonzales murder case, you wouldn't have connected it with your Jeweled Talon Society."

"Never crossed my mind. I knew Paula Tregarth had been murdered on her honeymoon by her wealthy groom four years ago. She was the mastermind of the Talons. All her idea. Paula was a true siren, vindictive to the core, but supreme at hiding her feelings and intentions behind a mask of sweetness and light. She couldn't stand her half brother, and hated her stepfather, who left her high and dry in his will. Marrying for money was her only recourse to sustain the lifestyle she craved."

"Who was the fifth Talon—the one our murderous captor thinks I am?"

Janice let out a small sound like a chuckle mixed with a moan. "Here's the kicker, sugar. I engineered for Kurt and me to move in next to you so I could do anything possible to help you and Caroline after April Hannover—the fifth Talon—stole your rich husband. Little did I know how glad you were to be rid of the jerk. You ended up being more of a blessing to me than I ever was to you. Without you and Caroline, I never would have survived the loss of Kurt or come into a personal relationship with God."

"April really is the fifth Talon? I thought she might be, but I couldn't be certain." Laurel snorted. "At least she made out like a bandit. Steven obligingly died in that boating accident and her ship came in."

"Knowing April, I always wondered how much of an accident Steven's death was."

Laurel's breath caught. How did she feel about the possibility that Steven had reaped what he'd sowed in the ultimate way? Sad for him—truly and deeply—but glad for the people he never had a chance to hurt. What a weird dichotomy. She would have much to sort out in her thinking…if she survived to enjoy that luxury.

The warmth seeping down to them from above had begun to wane. They must be huddled beneath a fireplace, and the fire was dying. Before much longer, Janice and she would be doing the same.

A drive that would take close to two hours overland took only a third of that by helicopter. Nor was a formal landing strip necessary in order to touch down in a parking lot of a small mountain town like Big Elk Meadows. The flash of generous green ensured the chopper and pilot could wait there as long as necessary for David to check out his hunch. Vehicle-rental agencies didn't exist in the little burg but more green bought the parking lot owner's rust-bucket four-wheel-drive SUV outright.

Fifteen minutes later, David turned in to the driveway of his mountain cabin. This cabin was the very one, according to the newspaper caption and photograph, where Lawrence Taylor murdered his bride four years ago. A detail David's Realtor failed to mention when she sang the cabin's praises and closed the deal.

Easing up the driveway, fingerling snow drifts went whump-whump under the SUV's tires, signifying that no other vehicle had passed here in a while. Tension sang in David's veins. If Lawrence had transported his prisoners by land, then the man hadn't been here. David was banking on the scenario appropriate to a man of Lawrence's resources—a willing hired brute of a pilot and an air approach.

The yard contained plenty of space for a helicopter landing, especially since the area had been cleaned out by the police-commandeered snow plow not many days ago. David would have preferred the swift approach himself, but dared not make so much noise and risk panicking the killer. Any miscalculation and Laurel and Janice could pay the ultimate price.

Please God, if my theory is all wet, and they aren't here, guide the police to the women. Please let it not be too late.

And how was Caroline? His gut churned. He couldn't even find out if she was hanging in there unless he had Laurel with him. He'd called but the hospital wouldn't tell a non-family member a thing.

He neared the end of the tree line. So far, the sound of the wind in the trees would have muffled his approach. A few yards more, though, and the car would burst into the clear and become visible from the cabin. He couldn't risk being spotted too soon.

David stopped the vehicle, but left it running. Brisk wind slapped his face as he got out. He moved on stealthy feet until he stood behind the last evergreen tree before the clearing. A long breath shuddered from his chest.

The packed few inches of snow left in the yard bore the clear indentations of a helicopter landing, but the bird was no longer there. The yard lay empty, and no lights showed in the cabin, though a wisp of smoke curled from the chimney.

David's knees went weak, and he sank into a mound of snow piled up against the tree's lowest branches. He was too late. The killer had been here with his victims, done his worst and gone. All that remained was for David to find what was left.

He couldn't do it. Fiery claws ripped at his heart. How would he face life without Laurel? When had she come to mean so much to him? The thought of finding her dead body—

David doubled over, a dry retch heaving his stomach. Heat flashed through him and sweat popped from his skin. He plunged his hand into the snow and rubbed a fistful on his face. The cold slapped him back to clarity.

He had no choice but to go inside and face whatever he might find.

David staggered to his feet and trod the distance

to the porch. A man trudging to his own gallows couldn't dread his destination more.

What would he tell Caroline? If she wasn't already with her mother.

The thought drove him to his knees on the top step, and the thud of his landing echoed hollowly. Then echoed again.

What?

David held his breath. Nothing. He shook his head. Grief was making him loopy.

He got up and tried the cabin door. It was locked even though the chimney smoke betrayed someone had been inside today. Anguish twisted David's face. He'd been here so seldom that having the lock changed after he purchased the property somehow got left on the back burner. Of course, Lawrence would still have a key to the place.

David pulled out his own key and let himself in. Gritting his teeth until his jaw creaked, he flicked on the light. His chest cavity went hollow. The place looked normal. No dead bodies. No blood. No smell of cordite as if a weapon had been fired. Just dying embers in the hearth. Why had the killer lit a fire? And what had he done with Laurel and Janice?

He strode to the fireplace and peered into the mass of glowing wood fragments. A few shreds of paper toward the back caught his attention. He grabbed the poker and pulled the scorched bits onto the hearth stones. A few traces of handwritten words showed around the edges, but not enough to offer a clue what the paperwork might have been. He gave the poker a frustrated shove into its container. The set of metal implements clattered together.

A hollow thump followed the clangor. This thump he hadn't imagined.

David stamped the floor, and the floor stamped back. His heart attempted to flail out of his chest. Someone was alive in the crawl space below. The temperature down there couldn't be much above what it was outside. Whoever it was—Laurel, Janice, both—must be freezing to death.

Where was that trapdoor? He'd seen it once beneath one of the thick oriental rugs.

David went into a frenzy of throwing carpets back from the hardwood floors. At last he discovered the spot in the corner of the dining room behind the piano. At sight of the shiny new padlock on the latch, David slammed the edge of his fist into the leg of the baby grand. He had no key for this lock.

Narrowing his eyes, David rose. He may not have a key, but he did have an ax outside in the wood box on the porch. No sounds had come from below since the thump he heard near the fireplace. Every moment counted. He ran for the tool. He'd chop up his entire floor if he had to do it, but it was best to work smart and fast.

He lifted the ax and brought it down on one of the trapdoor hinges. The hinges would succumb more quickly than the latch with its sturdy padlock. Again and again and again he struck at the hinges.

One hinge cracked and sprang loose. He attacked the other one. Strike! Strike! His muscles were energized. Fire pounded in his veins. He wouldn't fail Laurel. Not now. Not when he was so close.

A roar like muted thunder halted the upswing of David's ax.

Lawrence was returning? Did the vicious scum plan to finish with a bullet the job that he'd started by placing the women in the crawl space? No doubt the man had spotted the SUV sitting in the trees. David hadn't come armed. Maybe he should have, but he was a dreamer, a gardener and a piano man. When he'd scrapped as a snot-nosed kid, he'd done it with his fists. He didn't even own a gun.

The ax he held in his hands could serve as a weapon, but it was a feeble thing against a firearm. Nevertheless, it would have to do. He couldn't let that monster enter the cabin.

How much longer could the women last down there? He had to create the opportunity for them to reach warmth.

David brought the ax down once more on the second hinge. It sprang free of the wood. He grasped the edges of the trapdoor and ripped backward with all his weight and might. The latch bent and twisted. He heaved backward again, and the trap pulled open wide enough for someone to crawl out.

"Laurel!" he cried down into the dank and frigid blackness below. "If you can hear me, get out of there. I'm going outside to deal with Lawrence Taylor. Fire up the CB radio and call for help. I don't have time to do it."

Snatching up the ax, David raced to the front window. The chopper was settling to the ground in a swirl of white kicked up by the blades. There wouldn't be a better time to get out the door and take up a position of advantage behind Lawrence and the pilot, who would have their eyes on the cabin. Surprise might be his only advantage.

He raced down off the porch into the whirlwind of stinging snow particles and took up a stance facing the rear rotor blades of a sleek chopper, smaller but much nicer than the one he'd hired to fly up here. The whirling slowed and the snow began to settle.

David blinked and wiped at his eyes with his jacket sleeve. Then he drew back his weapon, primed and ready.

The view before him cleared, and the largely glass bubble of the main housing revealed one man inside. Lawrence was his own pilot? Certainly not out of the question, and the skill simplified matters greatly for a man bent on murder. The door of the chopper opened and a man toting a hefty handgun climbed out. Shock rippled through David. This was no stranger.

His entire understanding of the events of past years and prior encounters reshaped themselves even as new questions formed. Time enough for those later. The man with the gun took a step toward the cabin.

"Gil." David spoke softly, but in the cold stillness left in the wake of the silenced engine and rotor blades his voice rang clear.

"I see I was right to fear what my son might have communicated to you," Gilbert Montel said, not turning around. "You were so determined, and I couldn't be sure my silly sot act had fooled you."

"If I were in charge of the Emmys, you would win."

"Most gratifying." The man's breathing deepened as if in the grip of great emotion. "Lawrence killed my princess here." Gil waved toward the cabin. "I found him with her blood on his hands, babbling about the Society and her cruel contempt for men—especially him. The arrogant fool couldn't bear to think he'd been used. I killed him and tossed his body out there." He motioned toward the wilderness. "Now I must finish the task of eliminating the treacherous females who lured my princess into such a foolish pact."

"I have to stop you." David enunciated the words like hammer's blows.

Snarling a curse, Gil whirled. His gun lifted and barked even as David flung his ax. Something yanked his jacket sleeve, and he staggered back a step as Gil stared in wide-eyed shock. Bright crimson spread from the blade in his chest and the gun slowly lowered, then dropped to the ground. Gil's plump body crumpled and joined his weapon, lying still on the snow.

With a hoarse cry, David ran for the cabin and rushed inside. Laurel stood swaying near the trap-door—bleary-eyed and only half-conscious. Battered and bruised, Janice sat slumped against a wall. Both women quaked with violent shivers.

At his abrupt entrance, Laurel staggered, and David raced to scoop her in his arms before she could hit the floor. The woman was an icicle, but she was the best thing he'd ever held in his life.

"Oh, David," she wailed, "I thought he must have shot you. I couldn't bear it. I need you."

"I need you, too, sweetheart," he whispered fiercely into her precious ice sculpture of an ear.

Her sobs added to the shakes that quivered both their frames, but she lifted her face to his, pure joy radiating from her smile.

David covered that smile with his lips, and all chill fled in the warmth of her response.

EPILOGUE

Laurel joined hands with David, who joined hands with Caroline, who joined hands with her. In Laurel's refurbished dining room, they bowed their heads over an Easter meal prepared together with love and care. The savory scents teased her nostrils even as David's mellow voice pronounced the blessing.

She peeped between her lashes at the ginormous rock on her finger, and a smile grew on her lips. In only two months, she'd be a June bride. David would never have to leave for the night again. He would become one of those wealthy men content to lead an ordinary life in a middle-class neighborhood with his wife and child…and hopefully more children to come.

In the past few months, he'd proved a tremendous asset to the Single Parents Coalition, holding benefit concerts all over the country. His popularity had gone through the roof, at first from his spectacular acquittal in the public eye, summarized in a major newspaper headline: Millionaire Murderer at Last Exposed—But Not the One We Thought. After that, David's skill on the ivories soon won the brand of acclaim he deserved and would have made his mother proud.

Laurel's glance went to Caroline, so intense and intelligent and growing so lovely at nearly fourteen. She sat with her eyes closed, lips slightly parted, peace glowing from her face. They had nearly lost her. The tracheotomy scar in her throat showed faintly but would continue to fade with time. David had begun the process of legally adopting Caroline, to both her and Laurel's delight.

The Montel boy had long since ceased to harass her in school, but only last week Caroline had come home saying he had changed a lot since his father's death and the furor over what the man had done. Humbled by the experience, Grant was becoming almost likable…but just as a friend.

Not only did the boy provide the clue that sent David to the rescue at the cabin, but he proved invaluable in unraveling a terrible tale of deceit and betrayal and murder. How awful for the child to suspect his father was doing despicable things and to be spoiled and neglected by the man at the same time. The combination wasn't designed to produce good character.

The night Grant bowled Laurel over into her bushes, he'd seen his dad sneaking out of Janice's house and was running away for fear his father would notice him lurking outside Caroline's place. During the investigation subsequent to Gil's death, Janice supplied the information that her dealings with Gil as Realtor and client had given him opportunity to make a wax impression of her house key. On one occasion, he'd distracted her long enough that he would have had opportunity to find the security system codes for her house and for Laurel's that she kept in her purse.

Armed with Janice's key and code he could enter her house at will, no doubt to find the most promising poison on the premises in order to murder Melissa Eldon, but also to make a wax impression of Laurel's house key. Testing verified Gil's fingerprints all over the contents of Janice's purse, as well as wax traces on Janice's house key and the key to Laurel's house that was in Janice's possession. Getting into Laurel's car had been as easy as sneaking into her house, finding the car unlocked in the garage and tripping the trunk button.

How creepy that someone with evil intent had gained total access to their homes. Laurel still shuddered at the thought.

That ghastly day at the cabin, Gil Montel believed his plan was finally reaching its climax. By burning the papers from his loose-leaf journal he thought he had destroyed the record of all he had done, along with the last of the Talons. He succeeded in none of those things. Thanks be to God!

Besides Grant's and Janice's testimony, the housekeeper proved to know a great deal more than she liked, partly due to astute observation and partly because of her employer's habit of bizarre raving when he drank too much—which was often. She'd always assumed the comments to be morbid fancies, but now she knew they were likely true.

While Gil idolized his beautiful half sister, Paula, she treated him with contempt, which only seemed to feed his unhealthy fixation. When she married Lawrence Taylor, even though Gil was already married and had a child, he was heartbroken and eaten up with envy.

On the last day of his sister's honeymoon at the mountain cabin, where the couple was staying minus cell phones or other communication devices, Gil flew up there on the pretext of letting Paula know that an aunt had passed away. The rest of the story, sketchy as it was, David was able to supply from Gil's confession to him at the cabin.

Because of the interstate nature of the crimes Gil had committed, the FBI became involved in the hunt for Lawrence Taylor's remains. Employing modern technology combined with old-fashioned hound sniffing, they recovered teeth and bone fragments that verified Lawrence Taylor's actual fate, as opposed to the assumption that he was still at large.

After Paula's death, Gil began a vendetta to discover and wipe out the other Talons, who he blamed for involving his sister in the pact that got her killed.

Alicia became the first target when he glimpsed the tattoo on David's girlfriend as she whisked David away from him at the bar after the symposium.

With David and Alicia's party lifestyle, it wasn't difficult for Gil to disguise himself and pose as a hotel room-service waiter. The mickey he slipped into the champagne was both undetectable after a short amount of time and effective in putting them both out cold for long enough to dispose of Alicia. A supply of the drug was found during a search of Gil's estate.

Other types of drugs were also found, like the gases he rigged into the trunk of several of his numerous cars. One emitted deadly potassium cyanide, turning the trunk into a giant killing jar. Fiber analysis confirmed that Melissa Eldon met her end there.

Two other cars were rigged with sleeping gas. Once a person was placed inside, certain types of sounds and motions triggered the release of more gas upon a victim entombed in the trunk. After multiple doses, Caroline began to have an allergic reaction to it. Happily, the gas canister went empty at some point, which made all the difference between an extremely close call and certain death.

Laurel grieved the most over one outcome of the entire sordid mess—the loss of her best friend. Not that she and Janice weren't friends anymore. Yes, the truth had been hard to swallow, but Janice had been wrong to think that Laurel couldn't forgive.

They had meant too much to each other for too long for Laurel to hold the secrets of the past against her friend, even if those secrets had come home to roost in ways that endangered her and Caroline.

But Janice had been so traumatized that she left Denver—at least for a time—to seek peace of heart and mind by immersing herself in the renovation and disposal of a property she'd recently inherited from an obscure family connection. Laurel had the sense that she'd only scratched the surface of the secrets in her friend's past. She prayed that Janice would seek God's help in laying those heartaches to rest.

"Amen!" pronounced David.

His fingers loosened around Laurel's palm, but she tightened her grip and met his gaze with a broad smile. He grinned back, then tugged her nearer and pressed a tender kiss on her lips.

"Yummy," David pronounced, and Laurel's face warmed pleasantly.

Caroline giggled. "You lovebirds may be able to live on kisses, but I need solid food." She grabbed the bowl of mashed potatoes and wrinkled her nose as she gazed at the fluffy white mound.

"What?" Exasperation leaked into Laurel's tone.

Her daughter met Laurel's eyes. "If my eyes aren't playing tricks on me, I don't spy any lumps in your mashed potatoes. Have you been taking cooking lessons?"

David chuckled as Laurel shook her head

with a grin. "Just goes to show you should never make assumptions about people. We surprise you when you least expect it."

* * * * *

Dear Reader,

What a wild ride for Laurel, David and Caroline. As a writer, they were an endearing group of characters to work with, and I hope you enjoyed reading their story as much as I enjoyed writing it.

I have long been intrigued by the issue of how people choose to use their gifts and talents. Many who are born with great advantages in areas of looks or privilege, skills or finances, take these things for granted or as an entitlement. They choose to squander or misuse their gifts and end up causing themselves and others around them great pain and loss. On the other hand, many that are born into disadvantage grow up to lead extraordinary and noble lives.

Jesus is my greatest hero in this regard. He was born in a stable and raised as a laborer in an obscure village in a conquered nation. Scripture says He was an ordinary-looking guy—nothing spectacular about Him on the outside. Talk about excuses for low self-esteem!

Throughout his ministry He calmly and without compromise endured the condemnation of people who couldn't or wouldn't understand Him, and in His death submitted Himself to unspeakable cruelty. Yet in His brief earthly life He fulfilled every prophecy spoken of Him and changed the world forever! Anyone who puts trust in Jesus is given a new eternal destiny.

I enjoy hearing from readers so feel free to contact me through my website at www.jillelizabethnelson.com. You can also connect with me on Facebook at www.facebook.com/JillElizabethNelson.Author.

Abundant Blessings,

Jill Elizabeth Nelson

Questions for Discussion

1. Laurel Adams is a competent, educated and resourceful single mother who has been to the school of hard knocks and survived. Yet when her daughter begins exhibiting rebellious attitudes, self-doubt leads to frustration and fear. When people we love begin acting in ways that challenge us, how do we cope? What is a healthy reaction?

2. David Greene lives daily under a cloud of public judgment. He feels as if he's been sentenced to life in Solitary without going to prison. Have you ever sat in judgment on someone? What can we do to avoid making that mistake?

3. Have you ever felt condemned by the judgment of others? How should a person respond to unfair or ill-informed judgment from others?

4. Do we live in a society prone to making judgments about other people and situations? How much does the variety of available media contribute to mass judgment on a global scale?

5. Caroline Adams is struggling with some serious issues in her life, as well as issues common to teenagers figuring out their way to adulthood.

She feels smothered by her mother's protective instincts, and yet she isn't ready to manage all problems on her own. Does David handle her well? Why do you think Caroline bonds with him?

6. Laurel sometimes feels jealous over the way Caroline interacts with David. Why does she feel that way? What advice would you give Laurel?

7. David yearns for a family and a sense of belonging. He feels cut off and alone. At one point in his life, grief, as well as his sense of abandonment and rejection, caused him to behave recklessly and foolishly. What factors helped him turn his life around even though many of his circumstances didn't change?

8. Laurel reacts strongly to certain situations involving men she doesn't know or who she has reason to distrust. In David Greene, she feels she has encountered both. Are her responses understandable? Why or why not?

9. Best friends are one of life's special blessings. Laurel and Janice share a close friendship forged over common experiences and many years of association. Is that bond rendered any less real and enduring by the fact that a secret drove Jan-

ice to deliberately choose to befriend Laurel? Why or why not?

10. Every main character in the book has encountered major adversity in their past that has either changed them for the better or warped them. Have you observed this phenomenon in real life?

11. How have you responded to major tests in your past or present? Have you allowed adversity to develop your character or to warp you? Why is this a good question to ask yourself every once in a while?

12. What might drive women (or men) to make a pact that involves using natural gifts, such as looks or talents, to take advantage of other people? Do you see this "user" mentality in the world around you? Have you ever fallen into "user" behavior yourself in order to get something you wanted? How can we avoid being trapped into this mentality?

13. The theme scripture for this book is Proverbs 31:30. What does scripture say about the relative value of physical/natural things compared to spiritual/eternal things? Why is it so easy to get our value system turned wrong side out?

LARGER-PRINT BOOKS!

GET 2 FREE
LARGER-PRINT NOVELS
PLUS 2 FREE
MYSTERY GIFTS

RIVETING INSPIRATIONAL ROMANCE

Larger-print novels are now available...

LARGER-PRINT BOOKS!

GET 2 FREE
LARGER-PRINT NOVELS
PLUS 2 FREE
MYSTERY GIFTS

Love Inspired

Larger-print novels are now available...

ReaderService.com

Manage your account online!

- Review your order history
- Manage your payments
- Update your address

---

*We've designed
the Harlequin® Reader Service
website just for you.*

Enjoy all the features!

- Reader excerpts from any series
- Respond to mailings and
  special monthly offers
- Discover new series available to you
- Browse the Bonus Bucks catalog
- Share your feedback

Visit us at:

ReaderService.com